GAYLORD MG

Apocalypse
of the
Heart

Apocalypse of the Heart

BARBARA CARTLAND

GRAMERCY PRESS
New York

This 1995 edition is published by Gramercy Press,
distributed by Random House Value Publishing, Inc.,
40 Engelhard Avenue, Avenel, New Jersey 07001,
by arrangement with the author.

Random House
New York • Toronto • London • Sydney • Auckland

Printed and bound in the United States of America

Designed by Helene Wald Berinsky

Library of Congress Cataloging-in-Publication Data

8 7 6 5 4 3 2 1

AUTHOR'S NOTE

Amnesia means "loss or defect of the memory." It can be caused by any number of reasons, from a medical condition to a fall or a blow on the head. It can last a matter of hours or a few days, or there can be total loss of memory.

When total loss occurs, it might result in the patient having to relearn completely all that he had learned in childhood, from walking and talking to names of everyday articles such as "hairbrush" or "cat." This can be done very successfully, and the patient can make an almost total recovery.

In some cases the memory can return as quickly as it went, being triggered by something or someone very familiar.

1880

The Prime Minister bowed respectfully from the doorway.

Queen Victoria looked up with a smile.

"Good morning, Prime Minister," she said.

"Good morning, Your Majesty," he replied, bowing again.

The Prime Minister produced numerous papers and read them to the Queen, who listened attentively. Several Statesmen in the past had thought they could skip through the papers under discussion and Her Majesty would not notice. Queen Victoria, however, was determined to know every detail of what occurred in the Houses of Parliament, as well as the news from abroad.

It was not surprising that the British Empire was respected from one end of the world to the other. A great amount of it was due to the interest, the attention and the brains Queen Victoria brought to it.

The Queen and the Prime Minister spent an hour going over difficulties that were occurring in France, Germany and Russia, then the Prime Minister said, "I am afraid, Your Majesty, I have another request from the Balkans."

"Oh, not another one!" Queen Victoria exclaimed.

"I knew it would distress Your Majesty," the Prime Minister replied, "but as a matter of fact, Prince Lintz is of considerable importance and has proved himself to be a very forward-looking Monarch."

He paused, but when the Queen did not speak he went on, "As Your Majesty knows better than anyone else, his country is of such importance because it is on the edge of Russia."

"I am aware of that," the Queen answered.

"If it falls into Russian hands," the Prime Minister continued, "it will make things very difficult for us, especially for the Secretary of State for Foreign Affairs."

"I am aware of that, too," the Queen said sharply. "At the same time, I have no more relations, and no one can say that I have not done my best to provide the Balkans with more Union Jacks to fly over their Principalities than anyone else could do."

"As always Your Majesty has been absolutely brilliant," Mr. Disraeli said. Even though the other Statesmen sneered at him, he invariably flattered the Queen, and she enjoyed every word of it. He had a way of handling not only women but men as well.

Benjamin Disraeli, Earl of Beaconsfield, was the first Prime Minister to be so described in an official document. This recognition came in the signing of the Treaty of Berlin in 1878, which he signed as: *Beaconsfield First Lord of the Treasury and Prime Minister of Her Brittanic Majesty.*

"Your Majesty has been wonderful," the Prime Minister continued. "All the same, I would be very distressed, as I know Your Majesty would be, if Rasgrad fell into the hands of the Russians."

"They are behaving disgracefully, as you well know," the Queen said. "As I have said before, if I were a man I would go and fight them myself."

The Prime Minister had heard this many times. He merely answered, "And of course Your Majesty would win. But unfortunately the Russians are being very clever in infiltrating the Principalities and then going in to restore—as they say—Law and Order."

The Queen sighed. After a short silence she said, "Have you any suggestions to make? Because I have run out of nieces, nephews and, of course, Grandchildren."

"I expect Your Majesty knows who is called the 'Matchmaker of Europe.' "

The Queen laughed, as he had meant her to do. "There is many a true word spoken in jest," she said. "I have certainly kept a number of small countries secure. Whereas, if I had not done so, the Russians would have taken over and made their Empire even larger than it has become already."

With difficulty the Prime Minister prevented himself from saying what really worried him—India. But he knew it was a great mistake to talk of too many difficulties at the same time.

He, therefore, said slowly, as if he was afraid of upsetting Her Majesty, "There is still one relative to Your Most Gracious Majesty whom I think you have forgotten."

"Forgotten?" the Queen questioned. "Whom have I forgotten?"

"Your Goddaughter," the Prime Minister replied, "Lady Frederika, who I find bears your name together with two others."

The Queen stared at him.

"Of course I had forgotten her! How foolish of me! Is she old enough to be married?"

"She will be nineteen next Birthday," the Prime Minister said, "and, of course, Your Majesty remembers her Grandmother was Princess Frederika of Saxe-Coburg and Gotha."

"Then she was a distant Cousin," the Queen said. "But as she was so much older than I, I have no recollection of her."

The Prime Minister did not say he had researched the Family Trees of a large number of British Aristocracy and by chance had found that the Duke of Templeton had a daughter who was old enough to be married.

There was silence for a moment or two, then the Queen said, "The Duke of Templeton has always been a most respectful and, I think, intelligent man. But, as he spends most of his time in the country, unfortunately he has not visited me for a long time."

"Then if I may make a suggestion," the Prime Minister said, "it would be very gracious if Your Majesty sent for him and told him that the Prince of Rasgrad has asked for a Bride." He paused before he finished, "I am sure when he learns of this new discovery, the Prince will be very impressed and delighted to be connected with your Family."

"So he should be!" the Queen said sharply.

"It is the greatest honor Europe could have at the moment," the Prime Minister said. He hoped the Queen was listening as he continued, "Every Principality is longing for a British Bride to protect them against the Russians and to lift their status much higher than it would be otherwise."

The Queen was not aware of this. She was not giving it her entire attention. She was thinking, instead, it was strange that she had forgotten the Duke of Templeton. She herself had been wondering where next she could find a Royal relative.

She always resented it if the members of the Aristocracy did not call on her at least once or twice a year. Now she was thinking that the Duke had not been to Windsor Castle for at least four or five years. She had to admit, however, that he had been widowed about that time and had retired to the country. As far as she knew, he had never even attended the Sessions at the House of Lords.

"What I must do," she said aloud, "is write to the Duke and ask him to visit me and, of course, to stay for a night or two in the Castle."

"I am sure His Grace would be extremely gratified to hear from Your Majesty," the Prime Minister said. "It would, of course, have already occurred to Your Majesty that it would be a mistake to include Lady Frederika in the invitation until you found out a little more about her."

The Queen nodded her agreement as the Prime Minister went on, "If she is so young, one wonders whether she will be intelligent enough to realize what an important position is being offered to her."

The Queen was well aware that this was good sense. She and the Prime Minister had, in fact, recommended one girl as a prospective Bride to a Bulgarian Prince only to find that she was very plain and badly educated. They were quite certain after they met her that she would do more harm than good to any Royal Principality.

The Queen now agreed that she would write to the Duke herself. She would make sure it was impossible for him to refuse the invitation, but would not yet extend her hospitality to his daughter.

"Find out all you can about the girl," the Queen said. "I remember seeing her when she was about nine or ten and thinking she was an extremely pretty child. But, of course, her Mother was a great beauty."

"She certainly was, Your Majesty!" the Prime Minister agreed. "I remember meeting her soon after she was married to the Duke and thinking she was, without exception, the most beautiful woman I had ever seen."

"Then let us hope," the Queen said, "that her daughter takes after her. As we know from bitter experience, children often resemble the ugliest relative rather than the most beautiful one."

The Prime Minister laughed. "That is true! But of course every English girl wishes to be as beautiful as Your Majesty was when you came to the Throne."

The Queen smiled because she always enjoyed compliments when they were paid to her. No one was more clever than the Prime Minister in saying exactly the right thing.

"Now you are not to keep me talking," she said to him, "as you did the other day. We were reminiscing of when I first came to the Throne and forgot there was a deputation waiting impatiently outside."

The Prime Minister laughed. "Let them wait, Your Majesty. They are very lucky that you will listen to them whether it is first thing in the morning or last thing at night." He paused for a moment and then finished with, "As you well know, there is no other Monarch who is as kind and understanding as Your Majesty."

"I think it was Prince Albert who told me I must always help people when they need it," the Queen said. She gave a deep sigh before she added, "He never sent anyone away who wanted to talk to him and I still try, after all these years of loneliness, to carry out his wishes."

"As you well know, Your Majesty has been absolutely wonderful and the whole country is aware of it," the Prime Minister said. There was a pause, then he added, "Look how the Empire has expanded since Your Majesty came to the Throne!"

The Queen smiled and answered, "I am determined that even more of the world will, before I die, sing our National Anthem."

"I am sure that will come true," the Prime Minister exclaimed, "and we can rely on Your Majesty to make sure the countries over which Your Majesty now rules are well protected!" With that he bowed very low and began to walk backwards towards the door. He was delighted to think that he had persuaded the Queen to send yet another Royal Bride to a Balkan Prince.

The Queen had realized, even before he had, that she was running out of relations. She had thought the Balkan Princes would have to defend themselves since there was not another Royal relative left unmarried.

15

The Prime Minister had stayed up late at night in his efforts to find someone suitable, reading *Debrett's Peerage* and a number of other books which were concerned with European Monarchs. It was only by chance he had remembered that the Duke of Templeton's only daughter was a God-daughter of the Queen's. To be honest he would not have known it then if he had not seen that her names in *Debrett* were Frederika Alicia Victoria.

A great number of children were at the moment being christened after the Queen because she was so popular. It had, therefore, taken some time to realize that the Duke's Mother had been Princess Frederika of Saxe-Coburg and Gotha.

As he left the private rooms of Queen Victoria, he was congratulating himself on being very clever. He was determined that the Russians should not have more Balkan Principalities than he could help. But it was becoming more and more difficult to protect them from the greed of the Tsar, who was intent upon making his Empire at least double the size it was when he had first come to the Throne.

"Well, I have done him out of one more country," the Prime Minister said to himself as he got into his carriage to ride back to London. He knew when he arrived at Number 10 Downing Street that the Secretary of State for Foreign Affairs, the Marquess of Salisbury, would be waiting for him. The Marquess was very worried about the Tsar's position in Europe. He would now be delighted at what had transpired.

On the other hand, the Duke of Templeton was absolutely astonished when three days later, at breakfast, he read a letter which had been delivered that morning.

In fact, he read it through twice before he could believe it had actually come from the Queen. He thought, at first, it was some strange joke. It had been so long since he had been at Windsor Castle that he had forgotten he should pay an occasional visit to Her Majesty. Considering that his Family, the Templetons, were related by blood to the Queen, he had been rather rude.

In recent years, the Duke had spent most of his time in the country and was not particularly interested in his Family Tree, which he took for granted. He had actually forgotten that his Mother, who had died when he was quite young, was Royal. He found it difficult to remember now that she had come from a Foreign Family.

In fact, he always thought of himself as a good

English Aristocrat. He attended to his people and played his part in the County where he lived.

Templeton Priory had been in the Family since the reign of Queen Elizabeth. It started off as a Monastery, then generation after generation added to it. It became an extremely impressive house which was the pride, not only of the Duke's Family, but of all his neighbors.

The Duke had never cared particularly for London and, therefore, had not made the arduous journey from Yorkshire, except when absolutely necessary. Fortunately, it had not been necessary for the last five years or more.

He had become, in fact, the perfect English sportsman. He had his own Pack of Hounds and his own Shoot, which was an excellent one. He owned a few Race Horses with which he was quite content to win at the local Meetings and not attempt the more important ones.

The Duke was exceedingly kind to his Family, of which he was the Head. They turned to him for help and guidance in their problems, and he never failed to assist them.

After his wife died, one of his sisters helped him run the house and look after his daughter, whom he called by her second name, Alicia. In every way

she resembled her Mother. She was not only beautiful but extremely intelligent.

The Governesses who had taught her could not
speak too highly of her. "She has so many talents,
Your Grace," the last one had said to the Duke
before she left. "She is very musical, as Your Grace
knows, and plays the piano almost as if she were a
professional." The woman spoke enthusiastically.

But the Duke looked down his nose and said,
"That is one thing she will never be. I think it is a
mistake to be overcultured."

"Oh, Your Grace, I did not mean it that way,"
the Governess had said. "But she is so quick. Like
Your Grace, she loves riding. And, as I have often
said, she teaches herself as much as she learns
from her other Tutors and me."

The Duke, because he thought it was his Duty,
had engaged quite a number of local people to
teach his daughter. In the same way, he had been
taught himself at a Public School.

Other girls of Alicia's age were educated by a
single Governess who knew little more than they
did. Alicia, however, had top teachers, if they were
available, on practically every subject. She had
learned French from a Frenchman, German from
a German and Spanish from a Spaniard.

She had also, because her Father had found him after he retired, been taught history by an Historian, Sir Gerald Taylor. He had been at a University until he retired, and had also written a book on the Kings and Queens of England.

Because Alicia loved music, the Duke had found a musician, William Pate, living only five miles away who had retired after being in charge of the Choir, as well as the pupils, at Edinburgh University.

Alicia had loved the music he played to her, some of which he had composed himself. She had learned not only to play the piano but also to sing. Mr. Pate had taught her to sing as he had learned when he was a young man. He had, in fact, often told his friends that his pupil's talent was wasted in the Yorkshire Dales and that if she were in London, or any Capital City, she would be hailed as a brilliant singer and composer.

The Duke, however, took it all for granted. He was determined his daughter should be well educated, unlike most girls at the time. However, he had not been particularly interested in her achievements once she had accomplished them.

He liked her to sing for him in the evenings when they were alone. She played the piano to express herself at any time of the day, and sometimes he listened. More often, he told her to go out in the sunshine and exercise the horses.

"I am exercising my fingers, Papa," she had said once.

"You cannot win a race with them," he had told her.

"And you cannot expect your horses to be particularly musical," Alicia had answered.

Her Father had laughed. "We might try to persuade them to dance as you do. But I think they would be happier taking the new jumps I have erected on our Race Course."

"And I will race you over them tomorrow, Papa," Alicia had said, "and make sure I am the winner!" Again, her Father had laughed.

At the same time, he thought it was a mistake for his daughter to be too busy in the Stables, so he had found another teacher, Scott Ross, who had taught her to swim in the huge lake on the grounds of the Priory. He also taught her how to handle a canoe, which her Father had bought for amusement.

It had been a great sadness to the Duke that Alicia was an only child. He had considered marrying again simply to have an heir. But he had not, in fact, found anyone as beautiful or as charming as his wife had been.

Although quite a number of women had pursued him, he still remained a rather lonely widower. If he had found a wife (doubtless he would have no problem because he was so handsome), she would have taken him to London. She would make him entertain the *Beau Monde,* as he should have done for years. But he was quite happy and content in the country with his daughter to talk to him.

Members of the Family continually invited themselves to the Priory. He, therefore, had not bothered about the world outside his own little world.

Now the Queen's letter asking him to go to Windsor Castle not only took him by surprise, it also made him think. Because he was a very intelligent man, he wondered if perhaps he had been missing something of interest, something which was happening outside his own domain.

When his daughter came in from riding and joined him at breakfast, he showed her the letter.

"From the Queen, Papa," Alicia exclaimed, "how smart! I have never known her to write to you before."

"I have never known her to ask me to Windsor Castle before!" the Duke replied. "I have stayed there, of course, but always at the invitation of one of Her Majesty's entourage, not because of a letter like this, written in her own hand!"

"Then, of course, you will have to go," Alicia said. "It is so very exciting for you."

"Not as exciting as all that," the Duke said. "It means we will have to open the house in Grosvenor Square. It has been closed for a long time, although some of our relatives did use it when they had nowhere else to go."

Alicia laughed. "You are underrating your importance, Papa," she said. "They wanted to stay in Grosvenor Square because it made them feel so smart and important when they told their friends they were at Templeton House."

"I should think the place is pretty shabby by now," the Duke said. "Your Mother insisted on it being very clean and tidy, and, of course, massed with flowers."

Alicia, who had heard this before, said, "I love flowers just as Mama did and if you go to London, I will make sure you take plenty of flowers with you. Otherwise, you will perhaps feel cold and uncomfortable."

"If you think I am going alone," the Duke answered, "you are making a mistake. *You* are coming with me. I am quite certain that once we arrive we will be overwhelmed by invitations whether we want them or not."

Alicia stared at him.

"I can hardly believe what you are saying, Papa," she said. "Whenever I have suggested going to London before, you have always said you are quite happy here."

"That is true," the Duke murmured.

"You also said," Alicia continued, "you do not want me to be mixed up with a lot of tiresome young men who would only be interested in me because I was your daughter."

"Nonsense! I do not believe I said that," her Father replied. "Anyway, you will doubtless need some new clothes, and we have to go to London for those."

He paused before he added, "Of course, we must give a few parties, and you must go to a number of Balls."

Alicia laughed. "Are you going to escort me? I know how you hate Balls."

"I used to be a very good dancer," her Father said. "It is only now when I have to sit with the Dowagers and hear all the scandal of the County that I much prefer to stay at home and play Bridge."

Alicia laughed again. She knew her Father's pe-
culiarities only too well. Yet it had not worried her
that last year when she was a debutante he had not
wanted to take her to London. Instead, they had
given a Ball at the Priory which had been a great
success. She had, of course, attended a number of
other Balls which she had enjoyed because she
liked dancing.

At the same time, she shared her Father's delight in riding a fine horse. In fact, she preferred
galloping over the Yorkshire moors to doing anything else.

When she went upstairs, she was thinking that it
would be a wonderful new experience to go to
London, to meet people she had not met before
and to go to the Theatre.

The one thing she had wanted to do, because
her teacher had spoken so fervently of it, was to
see the dancers at Drury Lane and to hear the
singers at some of the other Theatres. She had all
the popular songs sent to her in Yorkshire, but it
was not the same as actually seeing the performance for herself.

Her Aunt Mary, who was as surprised as Alicia
had been at the letter from the Queen, was not
particularly keen to go to London. However, she
said to Alicia, "Of course, I must make the house

comfortable for your Father. As it has not been opened for so long, I expect the servants have been forgetful and the whole house needs a good cleanup."

"Then they had better do it before we arrive," Alicia said.

"I have every intention of seeing to that," her Aunt replied. "I am sure you will think it sensible of me to send down some of our senior servants to put things in running order before your Father gets there and, of course, you and I."

Alicia laughed and said, "Perhaps, after all, it is good for us to have new ideas and new friends. As it happens, Papa cannot say that it is we who are dragging him to London but the Queen."

There was a great commotion over the next few days before the Duke set off for London. He went by train, although he said he had always in the past managed to reach his destination by road.

"You have to move with the times," Alicia said. "The trains are so good now that there is seldom an accident. And everyone enjoys getting there in half the time it would take if they were taking the carriage."

"Whatever you may say, I prefer horses to engines," the Duke had answered.

"And I prefer them, too," Alicia said. "But on this occasion, as we are all going South, you must try the train and see if, after all, it is not a better and quicker way of getting there than the road."

To her Aunt, Alicia said, "I think actually, Aunt Mary, it is very good for Papa to go to London and, of course, to be invited to Windsor Castle. I have heard so much about the Queen I would love to meet her myself."

"I am sure she will ask you after she has seen your Father," her Aunt replied. "After all, she is your Godmother and you were christened with her name as well as the one your Mother chose for you."

"Three names are certainly a mouthful," Alicia answered, "and I am so glad that Mama liked Alicia."

"It is a very pretty name," her Aunt said. "At least there is no reason for you to use Frederika and Victoria. Make sure your friends, as you always have, address you as Alicia."

"I have no wish to be called Frederika, which I think is an ugly name," Alicia said. "But, of course, I must not say that about Victoria."

Her Aunt held up her hands.

"Certainly not! I am sure Her Majesty would be exceedingly annoyed if you were not humbly grateful to be named after her. It was a great delight to the Family when she offered to become your Godmother."

"She offered!" Alicia exclaimed. "Why did she do that?"

"I think, if you ask me, it was because your Mother and Father were such an attractive couple when they first married," Aunt Mary replied. "Your Father was tall and handsome, and your Mother was absolutely beautiful."

She gave a sigh before she went on. "Everyone said they were the most outstanding couple in the whole of the Social World. And I have always been told that the Queen has a great liking for very handsome men."

Alicia laughed, then said, "She has certainly mourned her own husband more than any other woman has ever done. She still wears black for him, and one of my teachers—I forget which one —told me that when she speaks of Prince Albert, the tears come to her eyes."

"She has been extremely faithful to him," Alicia's Aunt answered. "Although I am told she loves having men around her, she has never thought of marrying again herself in spite of the fact she is called the 'Matchmaker of Europe.' "

"I have heard she is called that," Alicia said. "I

have always been sorry for those poor relatives who are sent off to marry some unknown man in the Balkans simply because they think that an English Queen will stop the Russians from snapping up their Principality."

"I agree with you," her Aunt replied. "But I am sure every one of them has been too frightened to complain to the Queen." She paused a moment before she continued, "They, therefore, have done exactly as they were told and been sent off to the Balkans tied up in pink ribbon like a Christmas present."

"Well, if they frighten the Russians because they are carrying the Union Jack," Alicia said, "then that is all that matters. My teacher who came to visit last week was telling me that he is going to write a book about it. He is quite certain it will be a best-seller!"

"That will not be surprising," her Aunt said. "At the same time, I do not think the poor Brides find it very amusing."

The next day the three of them left for London.

Alicia found when she arrived in Grosvenor Square that the house was just as comfortable as the Priory. The servants who had gone ahead had worked twenty-four hours a day to make it perfect for their Master when he arrived. The head gardener at the Priory had insisted they take a great number of flowers with them.

"It is a lovely house, Papa," Alicia said, when she walked around it. "I came here as a child but had forgotten how big it is and how comfortable the rooms are. You will have to spend more time here in the future."

"I will do nothing of the sort," the Duke said. "I like the country and am already missing the horses."

"Well, go to Tattersall's tomorrow and buy some new ones," Alicia said, "both for the Race Course and for ourselves."

"Tomorrow I have to journey to Windsor Castle," the Duke replied.

"Well, do not stay too long because you must not forget we have already promised to dine with the Duchess of Manchester tomorrow night. As it will be, I am sure, a very smart party, I am only hoping I will look good enough to do you credit."

"You do me credit whatever you wear, and whatever you do," the Duke said. He bent and kissed his daughter as he spoke.

Then she answered, "You always say such nice

things, Papa. I know why you were such a success as the handsome young man about town."

The Duke laughed. "Who told you that nonsense?"

"I did not have to be told it," Alicia replied. "But I assure you that everyone told me a million times how handsome you were and how everyone wanted to marry you, before you saw Mama."

"I fell in love with your Mother the moment I saw her," the Duke said. "You are very much like her."

"When I look at her portrait," Alicia remarked, "I feel no one could be quite as lovely as Mama was."

"That is what I thought," the Duke answered, "but actually you are a very good runner-up."

"Well, I suppose I have to be content with that," his daughter retorted.

They were both laughing as they walked into the Dining Room. The Cook had excelled herself to please the Duke. At the end of the meal, he sent her a complimentary message to say how much he had enjoyed dinner and he hoped to enjoy many more before he returned to the country.

"It is no use your trying to return too quickly, Papa," Alicia said, as the Butler left the room with the message. "The invitations are already pouring in. We might as well enjoy ourselves."

She saw a quick frown on her Father's forehead and slipped her hand into his.

"Please, Papa," she said, "parties or no parties, I want to go to the Theatre." Alicia had a pleading look in her eyes as she went on, "Let us creep away one night, as soon as possible, to Drury Lane and to the other Theatres which I have never visited, although I have read a great deal about them."

"We will do the lot," the Duke promised. "But first I have to find out what Her Majesty wants."

"You can be quite certain," Lady Mary said, "that she will want something. They all tell me that she keeps everyone running round one way or another." She put up her hands as she explained, "They shake when they walk up the stairs to her private rooms at the Castle, just in case she is sending them off to the end of the earth on some special mission."

The Duke laughed. "I am old enough and sensible enough," he said, "to say 'No!'"

"I hope you are speaking the truth," Lady Mary said. "Because Her Majesty, from all reports, can be very insistent."

* * *

Alicia saw her Father off the next morning. She thought she would soon have to buy some new clothes, especially if they were going to luncheon at Marlborough House.

The Duke had thought it only polite to notify the Prince and Princess of Wales that he was in London. He had received a letter the moment he arrived at Grosvenor Square, asking him and his daughter to luncheon.

"You can be quite certain," Alicia's Aunt said, "that your Father, at any rate, will be asked to one of His Royal Highness's evening parties. I am told they are exceedingly amusing. Of course, the most important person present is whomever His Royal Highness is in love with, at that particular time."

"You listen to too much gossip, Mary," the Duke said.

His sister laughed. "Do you suppose that anyone in London speaks of anything else?" she asked. "The Prince of Wales has been the chief topic of conversation ever since I grew up. His love affairs will, in years to come, fill a dozen or more books."

"I expect you are right," the Duke answered. "But I have always been very fond of the Prince, and I think it is extremely unfair and unkind of his Mother to not let him take any part in State Affairs."

"Do you really think he is interested in that?" Lady Mary enquired.

"I am quite certain that he is, now being older and wiser," the Duke replied. "But Her Majesty is determined that he shall take no part in running the Empire. He therefore spends his entire time chasing women."

"But he has a wife and five children," Lady Mary retorted.

"I am aware of that," the Duke said. "But I understand that with his energy he actually wants something more to fill his days than chasing a pretty face who inevitably succumbs to anything he demands."

"When you put it like that, Papa," Alicia said, "it is really rather sad. Of course, as the Prince becomes King when the Queen dies, he *should* be allowed to take part in ruling the country now."

"I agree with you," the Duke said.

"He has not been allowed," Alicia went on, "or so they say in the gossip papers, to even look into the State boxes where the Queen keeps all the secrets of Europe hidden."

The Duke laughed. "I wonder if it is really as bad as that?" he asked. "But he has certainly gained an extremely bad reputation. I am not sure if I ought to take you to Marlborough House."

"If you leave me at home," Alicia cried, "I will scream by the front door until they let me in! I am longing to meet the Prince of Wales, and also the Princess."

"I will think about it," the Duke said. "But I am told that when I go to White's Club I will hear the latest gossip about His Royal Highness. The last two or three pieces I heard were not particularly to his credit."

"You are as bad as the Queen, Papa," Alicia said. "You condemn him without hearing his side of the story. I should be very upset if I were in his shoes and was told that everything that I wanted to know about our great Empire was secret and *verboten.*"

When she used the German expression, her Father laughed, and so did her Aunt.

"That is exactly the right word for it," Lady Mary said. "I have always thought it is a mistake to criticize Royalty, however badly they behave." She paused a moment and then went on, "You know as well as I do that gossip flies throughout the world far quicker than any bird. If we say one single word against the Queen, someone will go back to Windsor Castle and tell her what we have said."

"You are right there," the Duke agreed. "Alicia

must be more careful. I am afraid we talk far too freely amongst ourselves when we are at home. Any criticism of Windsor Castle or Marlborough House will be exceedingly unwelcome."

Lady Mary nodded her head but did not speak.

"In fact, I suspect," the Duke continued, "we should be banished back to Yorkshire immediately and told not to come down again." He was joking but Alicia guessed there was a word of truth in what he was saying.

"I will be very, very careful, Papa," she promised. "But tomorrow night can we go to Drury Lane?"

"I promise you I will take you there. I have already booked a box."

Alicia gave a cry of delight. She jumped up, put her arms round her Father's neck and kissed him.

"That was very, very kind of you, Papa," she said. "I know we will enjoy it. I am told the dancers are superb. It is something I have always wanted to see."

"You will see it even if we are ordered to dinner at the Castle," her Father replied.

"I will hold you to that, Papa," Alicia said. "I know that going to Drury Lane will be one of my dreams come true."

2

As the Duke drove himself towards Windsor Castle he was wondering, as he had wondered ever since he had received the letter from the Queen, what she wanted. He had given up his interest in Parliament a long time ago. In fact, he seldom came to London because he was so content in the country.

He only hoped the Queen was not wishing to appoint him as one of her entourage at the Castle. In which case, even if it offended her, he intended to say "No!"

He had sent the horses ahead when he came down from Yorkshire. He could not bear to be in London and never get outside the busy streets, which always bored him. He liked to feel as free as he did in the country. He knew that if the Queen, or Alicia, for that matter, wanted him to stay long he must have his own horses to ride. He had, therefore, sent down four of his best horses so that he could ride with his daughter every morning.

Now as they got out of London and into the countryside, he thought that his team went brilliantly on what was a very good road. He supposed that, because it was used daily by the Politicians and other people of importance going to Windsor Castle, they had to keep it in better condition than some of the other roads.

At the same time, he preferred the narrow twisting lanes of Yorkshire. He enjoyed being in the fresh air and not overburdened with visitors.

He knew, now he was once again in London, that the knocker on the door would be raised every few minutes. A great number of people, including his relatives, would be calling on him and Alicia.

I suppose really I should have given her a Season in London, he told himself.

At the same time, because she seemed so happy in the country, it was a pity to take her away. As he thought that, he laughed at himself. Of course, he was being selfish. Of course, he was staying in Yorkshire because *he* liked it there and did not like London. But Alicia was so beautiful, he knew she would undoubtedly be one of the Beauties of the

Season if he stayed long enough for her to be asked to every party.

When he arrived at the Castle, he was met by an Equerry who said how delighted they were to see him. "It is a long time since you were last here, Your Grace. We were saying at breakfast that we miss you."

"Now you are flattering me," the Duke replied. "You know as well as I do, with all the interesting and amusing people you have here every day, one rather dilapidated Duke would not be missed."

He certainly did not look dilapidated as he walked up the stairs. He was six foot one inch in height. Because he took so much exercise, his figure was as good as when he was a young man. He had no idea that people behind his back always said it was strange that he had not married again.

Although his wife had been an outstanding Beauty, there were a great number of other women who were beautiful, too. They would certainly have welcomed his attention with open arms. As it was, he was perfectly happy in Yorkshire. He almost resented it when people called on him uninvited.

The Castle, he thought, looked exactly as it had when he was last there. In fact, he was thinking only the Equerries would have been changed as they got older. But perhaps the Queen would keep them on, long after they had lost the handsome looks they had when first appointed.

Outside Her Majesty's Sitting Room, there was another Equerry in attendance whom the Duke remembered and who was delighted to see him. "How could you leave us for so long, Your Grace?" he asked. "We have missed you. Her Majesty has often asked when you were thinking of returning to London."

"I was not thinking of coming back at any time," the Duke replied. "In fact, I am only here today because I have been sent for. I am very anxious to know the reason for it."

"I will see if Her Majesty is ready to receive Your Grace," the Equerry said. He opened the door and came back a few minutes later to say, "Her Majesty is ready."

The Duke followed him into the room, where he saw the Queen sitting in her usual chair.

The Queen's Sitting Room faced South. From the wide oriel window it commanded a fine view of the South Terrace, the Long Walk, the Home Park and the Great Park.

Nearly opposite the window was a mantelpiece

of white marble. Above the mantelpiece there was a mirror set in a cream-and-gold frame which matched the paneling of the room. There was a clock of Empire shape, flanked by a priceless pair of vases, two bronze military statuettes and a pair of fine candelabra.

In front of the fireplace there was a threefold screen and a long couch covered with luxurious cushions. There was also a table over which was flung an embroidered tablecloth. It was littered with piles of photographs and illustrated catalogues of Royal possessions. Behind the sofa stood an enormous round table of beautiful inlay which was, however, almost completely hidden by the fascinating confusion of books, photograph frames and bibelots of all kinds.

The Duke's first thought, however, was that Her Majesty looked very much older than when he had last seen her. She was wearing the same mourning robes she had worn when Prince Albert died.

"I am delighted to see you, my Dear Duke," the Queen said, holding out her hand.

The Duke moved towards her, bowed over her hand and then stood waiting for her instructions.

"You may sit down," the Queen said, indicating a chair a little way from her own. This was a special privilege, as the Duke knew. When she consulted her Prime Minister and the other Members of the Cabinet, they always stood.

The Duke, however, thought apprehensively that she was going to ask him something he did not wish to hear. Although he sat down, he was not at ease.

"It is a long time since you visited me," the Queen began.

"I know, Ma'am. But Your Majesty will understand that, as I live in Yorkshire, it is a long way from London. I have so much to do on my Estate, it is almost impossible for me to come South."

The Queen laughed.

"It is a very good excuse, but you know as well as I do that the reason you do not come South is because you prefer, as you always did, being in the country with your horses."

The Duke smiled. "It has always been, ever since I can remember, impossible to deceive Your Majesty," he said. "And the reply to that is, of course, 'Yes,' that is the truth."

The Queen laughed again. "At least you are honest about it," she said. "Now tell me about my Goddaughter. How is she?"

"She is very well and very beautiful," the Duke answered.

The Queen looked at him.

"Is that true? Is she as beautiful as her Mother was?"

"Just as beautiful," the Duke replied. "In fact, now that I think of it, I have brought a miniature of her for Your Majesty to see."

He felt in his pocket and brought out a small velvet box containing a miniature and passed it to the Queen. She took it from him and saw that he had not exaggerated. The girl was obviously just as great a Beauty as her Mother had been. In fact, she was very lovely.

"I am sure you are not exaggerating in what you said," the Queen remarked.

She smiled at him before she continued, "Now what I have to ask you is something I feel you will not like. At the same time, it is of great importance to us and even more important to the country in question."

The Duke listened. It had never occurred to him why she had sent for him.

"As you know," the Queen was saying, "I have been very worried about the Tsar of Russia's determination to enlarge his Empire." The Duke made no comment as she went on, "It was, of course, all started by Germany making its country very much larger than it has ever been, by taking over all other Principalities and making them, one by one, part of an Empire."

She spoke with a note in her voice which told the Duke how much she resented the way Germany had been enlarged. Before the Duke could make any reply she went on, "Russia is now doing exactly the same thing, as you must be aware— even in the wilds of Yorkshire."

The Duke laughed as if he could not prevent himself and said, "Even in the wilds of Yorkshire, Ma'am, we have newspapers. So I am well aware that Your Majesty has strengthened the Principalities in the Balkans by sending your Grandchildren and other relatives. I am sure they are grateful to you."

"They are very grateful indeed," the Queen replied, "as they should be. At the same time, I cannot manufacture Royal Princesses out of the air, and I am now, quite frankly, extremely short of young relatives."

"You have been magnificent," the Duke said. "Everyone admires you. I expect, Ma'am, you are well aware you are called the 'Matchmaker of Europe.'"

The Queen smiled. "I would be deaf, dumb and blind if I were not aware of it. I only hope the Russians are impressed, if no one else."

"Of course, they are," the Duke said. "I can only say, Ma'am, that Your Majesty has been absolutely brilliant in keeping them at bay. Even though we are, at the moment, getting news of their continued advance into Asia."

"It took me a long time to persuade Mr. Gladstone that what they were doing was dangerous," the Queen said sharply. "In fact, as you very likely know, I threatened to abdicate as Queen if he did not do anything about it."

"I heard about that," the Duke said. "I thought you were completely and absolutely magnificent in standing up to him as you did. It is entirely due to you, Ma'am, that the Russian Army drew back when they were only six miles from Constantinople."

The Queen nodded her head. "That was a great moment," she answered. "But if they had taken it as they intended to do, it would have been a disaster, not only for Constantinople, but for Europe."

"Of course, it would have been," the Duke agreed. "Every thinking person in this country and in Europe is grateful to you."

The Queen sighed. "I hope so," she said. "But now I have asked you here because I have a special problem."

"What is that?" the Duke enquired.

"Prince Lintz of Rasgrad is in danger of having his Principality, which is not far from Russia, taken from him unless I supply him with a Union Jack in the shape of a British Bride."

The Duke stiffened. Now, almost as if a bomb had exploded at his feet, he realized why he had been sent for.

"I have gone through the list of my relatives and, of course, those of my Dear Prince Albert," the Queen went on. "I find I really have only one left—your daughter."

"My daughter!" the Duke exclaimed. "I do not think of her as being of Royal blood."

"But, of course, you know she is," the Queen said. "Granted, Frederika was a very distant Cousin of mine. In fact, so distant that she and her Family are often not included on our Family Tree. But she had Royal blood, which your daughter inherited from her."

For the moment, the Duke could not think of a reply. Because his Mother had died when he had been a very small boy, he had never thought of her as being a foreigner. She was seldom spoken of in the Family today because very few were old enough to have known her. Neither were they particularly interested in her Antecedents. In fact, he had never mentioned her to the Queen when he was constantly at Windsor Castle. He had actually forgotten that she was a relative of Her Majesty's.

"I feel," the Duke said, having difficulty finding words, "that although Your Majesty's suggestion is very complimentary, my daughter would not wish to leave England and would not enjoy having to live in the Balkans."

"Prince Lintz is, I believe, a very nice young man and is not old, as a great number of other Princes were who came to me for help," the Queen said. "In fact, I understand that Rasgrad is a very delightful and prosperous country and much more up-to-date than a great number of the Balkan States."

The Duke drew in his breath. He was trying to think of a good reason why his daughter should not accept the Queen's invitation and how he could persuade Her Majesty that Alicia had no wish to leave him or to live abroad.

"I have already been told," the Queen was saying, "how much your daughter means to you and how close a relationship you have together."

She paused for a moment before she went on, "That is why, in case you feel lonely after she has left England, you must come to Windsor Castle. I have a special position for you in my entourage which I think you will find interesting." She could see clearly by the expression on the Duke's face that he was not impressed by this, so she went on quickly, "I have missed you. I have missed your brain and the amusing way you always see the funny side of things, even if they are disastrous."

The Duke would have spoken but the Queen went on, "Personally, I would love to have you back at the Castle with me."

Perhaps for the first time in his life, the Duke found it impossible to put his feelings into words. After an uncomfortable pause he said, "Your Majesty is very kind. I am deeply grateful for what Your Majesty has said. At the same time, I have no wish to lose my daughter, and on her behalf I want to refuse Your Majesty's most kind thought that she should marry Prince Lintz."

There was silence for a moment. Then the Queen said, "Do you really think—and no one has a better brain than you, Your Grace—that you can refuse me?"

The Duke looked at her. He knew as well as she did that it was an impossible thing for him to do. As Queen of England she was commanding him to give his daughter to Prince Lintz of Rasgrad. There was actually no question of his being able to

refuse what was a Royal command given to him by
Her Majesty herself.

Again there was silence. At last he said, "If I
plead with Your Majesty, would you listen?"

"No!" the Queen replied firmly. "Not because I
want to hurt you. Not because I do not know how
much you will suffer in losing your daughter. But
as you do know, Great Britain is more important
than individual feelings." The Duke shut his eyes
for a moment as the Queen continued, "The only
way we can prevent Russia from taking over yet
another Balkan country, which is very much to its
advantage, is that the one country it cannot afford
to fight at the moment is Great Britain."

The Duke knew only too well that this was true.
He was aware, as every thinking person was aware,
that only the Queen, having to fight her own
Prime Minister to get her way, had prevented Russia from invading and capturing Constantinople.
It had cost enormous sums of money and an even
greater number of lives of trained soldiers.

The Russians were now even more afraid of
Great Britain than they had been before. The
Duke knew quite well that if Russia could steal, one
way or another, more Principalities in the Balkans,
its position would be strengthened to the outside

world. The Russians themselves would be lifted up, feeling they were of more importance in Europe than they actually were.

The Queen did not speak but was watching the Duke. He knew that he was defeated without either of them saying any more.

With considerable effort, which made him feel as if it came from the very depths of his being, he asked, "How soon would you want my daughter to go to Rasgrad?"

"As soon as you can possibly arrange it," the Queen replied. "I am told that the Russians are already infiltrating the country. They are causing trouble in the usual manner, which will give them the excuse that they have used before: to go in to restore Law and Order." She paused a moment before she continued, "The Prince's Secretary of State for Foreign Affairs, who arrived here last week, told me they have produced more tricks than usual in their efforts to stir up trouble."

"I know very little about Rasgrad," the Duke said. "But I always imagined it to be a peaceful and happy little country."

"It was—until the Russians thought it important to them," the Queen said. She shook her head very slowly before she went on, "I understand that the Tsar is furious because Germany has become so large. He is determined, sooner or later, to take over the whole of the Balkans and thus pave the way to the Mediterranean."

The Duke had heard this before. There was nothing new about it. At the same time, he was aware that politically Her Majesty was entirely right. It would, therefore, be impossible for one man like himself to fight against her.

He was well aware that every country in Europe was applauding the clever way she had already saved so many of the Balkan States. Rasgrad was one of the most important of them. It was surprising it had not been threatened before.

Looking back, and it was difficult because he had been out of the political world for so long, he remembered that the Prince's Father had been a very strong and important Monarch. He had spoken out at the Foreign Conferences which had been held on both Russia and Germany. A large number of Diplomats had thought his defense of his own country would inspire other Balkan Royalty to follow him. That the Queen had now chosen the Duke's daughter to represent Great Britain in what was one of the most important problems of the time was, therefore, a compliment he could not ignore nor refuse.

Because he was powerless to protest, he could

only say, "I will, of course, convey Your Majesty's command to my daughter and I will, if that is what Your Majesty wishes, discuss the matter with the Representative of Rasgrad, if he is still here in the Castle."

"Of course he is here!" the Queen said sharply. "He has been awaiting your arrival anxiously. He said to me that it is essential that something be done immediately to prevent the Russian infiltration."

The Duke knew there was nothing more he could say. He rose slowly from his chair. Standing in front of the Queen, he said, "My Family has been loyal to the Crown and served it, in one way or another, for the last 400 years. I can only promise, Your Majesty, that my daughter will do her best to save Rasgrad from the Russians."

The Queen smiled.

"I knew you would understand how important it is. But I am sorry, Your Grace, to take your daughter from you. I am sure, now that the train service is so much better than it has ever been, you will not find it too arduous a journey to Rasgrad."

The Duke, aware that the Queen wanted the arrangements to be finalized as soon as possible, said, "I will talk to the Representative of Rasgrad, and, of course, I would like to say goodbye to Your Majesty before I return to London."

"Of course, of course!" the Queen replied. "I would be very hurt if you left without doing so." She held out her hand. In a very different tone of voice, she said, "I am sorry, very sorry to do this to *you*, of all people. I know it hurts you and you will miss your daughter. But I have always believed England must come first. We cannot fail those who rely on us."

The Duke bent over her hand. "Your Majesty is a very wonderful person," he said, "and, as I well know, Your Majesty always wins."

The Queen laughed. "That is what you used to say to me years ago. I only hope when your daughter is in Rasgrad that you will spend more time with me here at the Castle than you have done recently."

"Your Majesty is more than kind," the Duke replied. He bowed again, then moved backwards towards the door.

As the Duke reached it, the Queen said, "Come and see me before you leave for the marriage. I will be waiting to hear what you have arranged."

The Duke did not answer; he merely bowed. As the door opened behind him, he left the room. He felt so shaken that for a moment he could not speak.

The Equerry waited for some seconds before the Duke managed to ask, "Where is the Representative from Rasgrad, who I understand is here in the Castle?"

"He has been waiting to see you, Your Grace," the Equerry replied, "and I will take you to him." He walked ahead and the Duke followed.

Only when they came to a room which was some distance away from Her Majesty did the Equerry stop and say, "I have ordered a bottle of champagne to be put on ice, as I thought Your Grace might need it. Of course, we would be delighted if you could stay to luncheon."

"No, no. I must get back," the Duke said quickly.

It was not what the Equerry had expected. Without saying any more, he opened the door, announcing to a man sitting comfortably in one of the armchairs, "His Grace the Duke of Templeton."

The man jumped to his feet as the Duke came into the room and the door was closed behind him.

"I am Baron Gavrion," he said in fairly good English. "As I expect Her Majesty has told you, I am the Secretary of State for Foreign Affairs in Rasgrad."

The Duke walked to a table on which the champagne mentioned by the Equerry was in a gold wine cooler. He poured himself a glass before he asked, "Might I pour you a glass of champagne?"

"I have one, thank you very much," the Baron replied.

The Duke drank from the glass as if he needed the sustenance of it before he said, "As you expected, I have agreed with Her Majesty that my daughter will marry His Royal Highness."

The Baron, who had been looking very anxious, gave an exclamation of delight.

"That is splendid! That is excellent, Your Grace! It is of greatest importance to us in Rasgrad that we should have the support of the British Queen. As your daughter, Lady Frederika, is related to her by blood, you can imagine how honored and delighted our country will be." He was obviously so excited that it was difficult for the Duke to say anything except that he was glad to be able to help Rasgrad. They sat down.

Because the Duke was still suffering from the shock of losing Alicia, he made arrangements with the Baron as quickly as possible. He also accepted his request to talk things over the next day in

London. Having drunk the glass of champagne, the Duke rose to his feet.

"I am now returning to my house in Grosvenor Square, where you will be brought tomorrow at noon," he said. "I will then know more clearly my daughter's wishes in this matter and decide how soon the Wedding can take place."

"As quickly as possible," the Baron begged. "Things are very bad in Rasgrad. Russians creep in. We cannot keep them away. More and more Russians come every day into towns and the Capital, where the Palace is."

"I understand your difficulties," the Duke said quickly. "But I must find out more about His Royal Highness and when it will be possible for us to arrange the Wedding."

"Soon, soon!" the Baron said. "When Russians see an English Bride, they will run away."

"We can only hope so," the Duke said coldly. He put down his glass. "I will see you tomorrow morning at twelve o'clock," he said. "I am sure they will arrange to convey you to my house, where I will be waiting."

He shook the Baron's hand. While the Baron expressed his delight, the Duke walked towards the door.

He still could not believe that what had

happened was real, that he would lose his daughter to a Balkan State because it was threatened by the Russians. He had never, in his wildest dreams, thought such a thing was possible. Yet he could understand, because he had always been a Politician, that the Queen had found Alicia only by scraping the barrel, so to speak, of those eligible to represent Great Britain. "I do not know what she will say to this," the Duke said as he drove home.

Only when he was halfway to London did he remember that he had not said goodbye to Her Majesty as she had asked him to do. *She will have to excuse me,* he thought, *for what must appear an act of rudeness on my part, which is a result of shock.*

Of course, he was shocked. Of course, he had no wish to lose Alicia. He was almost certain that she would try to refuse the Royal Command to marry a man she had not yet seen.

How can I make her do anything so unpleasant? the Duke asked himself. He was, in fact, afraid of the answer.

Alicia had passed a most enjoyable day spending money. She had realized when she reached London that her clothes, though pretty, were really out of date.

Bond Street was filled with extremely attractive

gowns, which they said came from Paris. What was considered smart in Yorkshire was definitely dowdy and even in "bad taste" in London.

She bought herself three entrancing evening gowns, which made her look even more beautiful than she was at the moment. Day clothes were easier to buy, though not much cheaper. The colors which she loved and became her best, she thought, were the colors of the flowers which filled the garden at home.

As the afternoon ended, she found that she had bought more than she intended simply because the clothes were so beautiful. Each one seemed to her more becoming than the last. Of course, she had to have hats to match. Then she remembered that the shoes she wore in the country were not at all suitable in London.

Wearing one of the dresses she had bought with a hat trimmed in flowers to match, she found that, when she looked in the mirror, she had difficulty recognizing herself. *I am sure Papa will be thrilled with my appearance,* she thought.

She stopped on the way home to buy him a special present which she knew he had wanted for some time.

When she finally left Bond Street, she was late for tea. But she expected that her Father would have stayed at Windsor Castle longer than he intended. *It is very good for him,* she thought, *to be with the Queen again, and with the men Her Majesty invariably has around her.* Then she added aloud, "I suppose really Papa is wasting his brain staying in the country."

At the same time, Alicia knew only too well that he was happy at home. While she was in the Schoolroom, it had been difficult for him to help her Mother entertain. Her Aunt, who was a very sweet and gentle person, did not particularly like big parties. She, therefore, was only too willing to do as her Father wanted and have as few visitors as possible to the Priory. In fact, they would sometimes go for several weeks without entertaining anyone or accepting local invitations.

Now that I am grown up, I must make an effort to ask Papa's friends to stay with us, she told herself, *as well as some of my own.* When she thought it over, she decided she had very few friends. There were not many of the same age as herself near to the Priory in Yorkshire.

At the parties they had attended since they arrived in London, she had been astonished at the invitations she had received and the flattering things people had said to her. She was not stupid, and realized that, as her Father's daughter, she was of some importance. At the same time, it was almost a shock to come from the quietness of the country to the rush, dash and excitement of London.

Last night they had dined with a friend of her Father's who had a daughter the same age as herself. *She was, in fact,* Alicia thought without being unkind, *a rather plain girl.* But she had a number of her friends at dinner. Afterwards another lot arrived and they danced. There were only a piano and a violin, as it was not a large party. But Alicia found it very exciting. It was, of course, amusing and flattering when the young men fought to partner her.

They had not left until one o'clock in the morning. She would have stayed longer if her Father had not taken her away.

"If *you* do not want to go home," he said, "I do! Remember, I have to go to Windsor Castle tomorrow, and I will not be welcome unless I have all my wits about me."

"You always have that, Papa," Alicia replied.

"I am not so certain," the Duke said. "It puzzles me as to what Her Majesty is asking me to do."

"I think you are being stupidly modest," Alicia answered. "Of course the Queen wants to see you. You know how dull most Politicians are. I expect

Her Majesty is fed up with them and wants you there to make her guests laugh."

"It's been a long time since I have done that," the Duke said. "But, of course, I will try."

"You are always witty and great fun, Papa," Alicia said. "The only difficulty is that I find, compared to you, all the young men I have met so far seem very stupid and uninteresting."

"Nonsense!" the Duke exclaimed. "There was a very nice crowd of boys there tonight. Tomorrow night, when you dine at Marlborough House, you will meet a much older group and, of course, the Prince of Wales himself." He paused before he added, "There is no need for me to say you are not to flirt with him, although it is unlikely he will try to flirt with you."

"Why do you say that?" Alicia asked.

"Because he likes older women and, of course, has a bad reputation in consequence," the Duke answered.

"I am longing to meet him," Alicia said, "although you told me I had met him when I was only a child."

"I do not suppose you took much interest in my friends then," the Duke remarked. "But they always said you would grow up to be a Beauty, which you undoubtedly are." He had not missed the attention she had received at the party last night. He thought they would soon be talking about her in the *Beau Monde,* which undoubtedly included the greatest gossips of the whole Social World.

When Alicia reached Templeton House in Grosvenor Square, she saw the Chaise in which the Duke had driven down to Windsor Castle with its four horses. She thought with joy that her Father was back. He had been far quicker than she expected. She hurried into the house, telling one of the footmen to collect her parcels from the carriage before it was taken to the Mews.

"I am home, Papa!" she called out as she ran down the passage to his Study, where he always sat. She opened the door and found him, to her surprise, drinking a glass of champagne. As he very seldom, if ever, drank in the afternoon, she thought he must have felt hot and perhaps exhausted from the journey to Windsor.

She ran across the room and kissed him before she said, "I have spent a fortune on new clothes, Papa! I do not want you to be ashamed of me at all the parties we will undoubtedly be going to. I realized last night that I looked like a real country girl, which is not particularly complimentary."

She was laughing as she spoke. Then she saw

the expression on the Duke's face and asked, "What has happened? What is wrong? I know, Papa, something has upset you!"

For a moment the Duke did not answer, then he said, "Sit down, Dearest, I want to talk to you."

Knowing something strange had happened and wondering what on earth it could be, Alicia sat down in an armchair. She pulled off her hat as she did so and threw it down on the floor beside her.

"What has gone wrong, Papa?" she asked.

"I hardly know how to tell you," her Father answered.

"The Queen is not dead, is she?" Alicia enquired.

"No! No, of course not!" the Duke replied. "It is nothing like that."

"Then what has upset you? What can have happened at Windsor Castle, of all places, to make you look so serious? Or perhaps the right word is 'worried.' "

"Actually," the Duke said slowly, "I am worrying about you."

"About me?" Alicia enquired. "Why should you worry about me?"

"Because, my Dearest . . . ," he began, then walked across to the window. ". . . I do not know how to tell you this," he continued.

63

Alicia looked at him and for a moment found it difficult to know what to say. Something had deeply upset her Father, and as she looked at him staring out the window, she knew it must be something very serious. She wondered if she should run to him and put her arms round him, but he had told her to sit down and he always liked to be obeyed. Finally, he turned round and walked back towards her.

"When I got to the Castle," he said, "I was shown directly into the Queen's Private Sitting Room. She told me the reason she had sent for me to come to London was a very serious one."

"Serious for whom?" Alicia asked. "For the country or for you?" Alicia wondered vaguely if England were at war. Perhaps a close relative of the Queen's had died unexpectedly, but that, surely, would not particularly worry her Father. She could not imagine why he was looking as he did, or why he was taking so long to tell her what had happened.

"I do not know," the Duke said after a pause, "how to tell you this. But you must be aware—in fact, we have talked about it—how Russia is infiltrating the Balkans and gobbling up every Principality it can by saying it must restore peace."

"Yes, of course, I know all that," Alicia said,

"and we were both shocked at the way the Russians behaved."

"What the Queen has asked me," the Duke said at last, "is if you will go to Rasgrad and marry Prince Lintz, because they think that at any moment the Russians might take over that country."

"Marry the Prince!" Alicia exclaimed. She could not believe she had heard correctly what her Father had said. At the same time, she understood now why he was looking so upset. "But of course I cannot go to any Balkan country," she said, "and marry a man I have not even met."

The Duke gave a deep sigh.

"My Dearest daughter," he said. "It is a Royal Command. I tried to save you, but one cannot fight the Queen."

Alicia stared at him.

"Are you really saying, Papa, that I *have* to marry this Prince because the Russians are trying to take over his country?"

"That is what Her Majesty believes they will do, if he is not married to English Royalty," the Duke replied.

"But I am not English Royalty!" Alicia protested. Then she stopped. "Of course, I had forgotten Grandmama."

The Duke nodded.

"Before she married, she was Princess Frederika of Saxe-Coburg and Gotha and, of course, you were named after her. A distant relative but, undoubtedly, a relative of Her Majesty's."

"It did not cross my mind," Alicia said. "Oh, Papa, how can I possibly go to a strange country in the Balkans and marry a man I have never seen and who, very likely, does not speak English?"

"I expect he does," the Duke said. "At the same time, my Dearest, there is nothing we can do. Nothing!" Alicia did not speak, and after a moment he added, "All the way home I have been trying to think of a way out. But unless we battle the Queen, which is impossible and for which we could be imprisoned, we have to obey the Royal Command!"

"It is ridiculous! It is absolutely ridiculous!" Alicia cried. She got out of the chair and walked across the room. "How can I *possibly* agree to marry a man I have never heard of until now?" she protested. "And a man I have never met. He may be 180 years old, for all we know!"

"No! He is, I think, about seven or eight years older than you."

"It would not matter if he were ninety, if I knew him and liked him," Alicia said. "But being forced into marriage is absolutely ridiculous. It may have happened in the past but should not happen today."

"I agree with you completely," her Father replied. "But when I tried to argue, Her Majesty made it a Royal Command, and you know there is nothing we can say or do against that."

"Well, I would say a great deal if I had the chance," Alicia said. "But I suppose if I kick, struggle and protest, no one will pay any attention to me." The Duke did not answer. Then Alicia threw herself against him.

"Oh, Papa, save me!" she cried. "How can I possibly marry a man I have never met?"

The Duke put his arms round her and held her close. "I am afraid it happens to all Royalty," he said. "They have to marry for the good of their country and, in this case, to save a country. I do not suppose the Prince wants to marry you, any more than you want to marry him."

"That does not make things any better," Alicia said. "I think the whole thing is disgusting, disgraceful, and in a civilized world, it ought to be stopped."

"I agree with you," the Duke said. "But I do not know how to stop it."

There was silence, then Alicia said, in a very small, quiet voice, "What . . . can I . . . do . . . Papa?"

"Nothing, Dearest, except obey Her Majesty's command." His daughter did not reply, and after a moment he said, "The Secretary of State for Foreign Affairs is coming here tomorrow to make arrangements for us to leave for Rasgrad. You can talk to him and find out all the things I ought to have asked but was too shocked and upset to do."

He gave a sigh and then exclaimed, "Actually I forgot to say goodbye to Her Majesty as she had asked me to do! I just wanted to get away from the Castle and back to you."

"I had no idea when I was shopping happily in Bond Street," Alicia said bitterly, "that this was waiting for me at home."

"We must ask for time for you to get your trousseau," the Duke said, "and perhaps we will think of some solution, although I do not know at the moment what it will be."

"The only real solution will be if the Russians snatch the Prince away before I get there," Alicia cried. "In which case there will be no Wedding."

"I can hardly say that to Her Majesty," the Duke replied.

"No, of course not," Alicia said, putting her

fingers up to her eyes. "But I just cannot imagine how it is possible this should happen to me." She gave a tearful sigh. "I suppose I always hoped that one day I would fall in love with someone tall and handsome like you, as Mama did. She often told me how attractive you were and how you fell in love with her the moment you saw her."

"She was the most beautiful person I had ever seen," the Duke replied. "You are, in fact, my Dearest, very much like her."

"Then I cannot see why I should waste myself on some Balkan Prince who is not strong enough to save his own country from the Russians."

"That is exactly what he is trying to do," the Duke replied. "But unfortunately at our expense."

"Oh, Papa, I cannot do this!" Alicia cried. Now she moved close to her Father, and he put his arms round her as she hid her face against his shoulder.

"How . . . can I . . . leave . . . you and . . . the . . . horses and . . . everything I . . . love . . . in my . . . home?"

"You would have to leave me one day," the Duke said. "Only I had hoped you would meet someone who was worthy of you and who would love you as I loved your Mother."

"That . . . is . . . what . . . I . . . was . . . wanting . . . too, Papa, and . . . now it . . . is

. . . something I . . . will not . . . have!" She did not cry but shut her eyes to prevent herself from doing so.

Her Father held her very close. As he did so, he thought that of all the problems he had encountered in his life, this was the worst—one to which he could find no answer!

3

The Secretary of State for Foreign Affairs in Rasgrad, his wife and another woman arrived at a quarter past twelve.

The Duke and Alicia were waiting for them in the Drawing Room. Alicia was very pale. Her Father looked at her anxiously but thought it wise not to ask questions.

The Butler announced in a stentorian voice, "The Baron and Baroness von Gavrion, Your Grace, and Countess Udelana."

A gray-haired man, not very tall and with somewhat indifferent looks, came into the room. His wife, who was elaborately dressed but had a face it would be difficult to remember, was with him. Behind them, looking rather crushed, was the Countess, who was young but not particularly attractive.

The Duke, however, was very friendly. "It is

delightful to see you, Baron," he said, "and I hope you had a good journey."

"Very good, indeed," the Baron replied.

As they had luncheon, Alicia found that the Baron's wife and the Countess spoke broken English. The Baron, however, was delighted that Alicia, whom he called Lady Frederika, was to come with them to Rasgrad as soon as possible.

"You must give my daughter time to buy her trousseau," the Duke said. "She will naturally require many more clothes than she has needed in the country. I imagine you do a great deal of entertaining."

"His Royal Highness is very hospitable," the Baron replied. "He has as guests many important people from other countries." He gave a little laugh as he said, "He is determined they remember Rasgrad, even if we forget where they live."

"I think that is very sensible of him," the Duke replied.

"Her Majesty was telling me," the Baron went on, "you live in Yorkshire."

"Yes, indeed," the Duke answered. "It is very far away but we love being there. Of course, my daughter will miss her horses very much."

"Aha!" the Baron exclaimed. "His Royal Highness has very good horses, yes! He rides in the

morning, out of the City and among the mountains, which Lady Frederika will think very
beautiful."

The Duke thought his daughter looked a little
more cheerful when she learned there were horses
available for her to ride. At the same time, he was
aware she had hardly spoken since the Baron and
his wife had arrived.

"I have sent a cable to Rasgrad today," the
Baron went on, "telling His Royal Highness that a
very beautiful Bride has been given to us by Her
Majesty Queen Victoria. I know that tonight everyone in the Houses of Parliament will be celebrat-
ing."

Again the Duke glanced at Alicia, and he realized she was looking even more depressed than
she had been before the Baron had arrived. "I am
afraid," the Duke said, "I know very little about
your country. You must tell me and, of course, my
daughter how attractive it is."

"Rasgrad is very big and very beautiful," the
Baron replied. "Full of happy people whom we
want to keep happy."

The Duke could understand this but thought it
wise not to mention the Russians. He, therefore,
talked about his Family Estate and told them what
he remembered of his Mother, Princess Frederika.

"I was only six when she died," he said, "so you will forgive me if I can tell you very little about her."

"What is important," the Baron said, "is that Lady Frederika is the Goddaughter of Her Majesty Queen Victoria, in addition to having the Royal blood in her veins."

"Yes, of course," the Duke agreed. Turning to the Countess, he asked, "Are you living at the Palace at the moment, or have you been especially engaged to accompany my daughter to her Wedding?"

"I live in country, but I distant relative of His Royal Highness," the Countess replied. "But I not see much of him." She spoke very bad English. In fact, it was difficult to understand what she said.

The Duke turned to the Baron with a feeling of relief. "I had hoped," he said, "that you would bring photographs of His Royal Highness and, of course, the Palace."

The Baron threw up his hands. "Alas! How stupid of me," he said. "I never thought of it. Of course, it was very silly of me. Like Her Majesty Queen Victoria, we have many photographs. His Royal Highness finds photography a new toy."

"As we did when it first appeared," the Duke said. Again he glanced at his daughter. He was

aware from the expression on her face that she was
finding the Baron and his wife dull and unattractive as well as difficult to understand. Her Father
could almost read her thoughts: if she had to live
permanently with people like these, she would run
away.

"In the winter when the snow and the ice
come," the Baron was saying, "we ski and skate on
the lakes. But in the summer it can be very hot.
Lady Frederika must bring a sunshade with her."

"That is true," the Countess said. "I very bad
burns last summer. They spoil face."

The Duke wondered if that was why she looked
so plain. He thought someone at the Palace was
not being tactful in sending such a dull woman to
escort a young Bride.

After luncheon when Alicia was reluctantly taking the Baroness and the Countess round the
Picture Gallery, the Duke was alone with the Secretary of State and able to ask him questions which
he wanted answered.

"As I understand it," he said, "His Royal Highness is twenty-seven. I wonder why he has not
married before."

The Baron smiled. "I tried to persuade him do
so but he was determined to enjoy himself."

"Where did he do that?" the Duke asked.

The Baron made an expressive gesture with his hands. "Everywhere he could," he replied. "Paris, Berlin, Cairo, Athens! The map is always open."

"I can understand that," the Duke said.

"We talk and talk and ask and ask," the Baron said, "but His Royal Highness says, 'No! No! No!' We get no further."

"Then why has he changed his mind?" the Duke asked.

The Baron shrugged his shoulders, then said, as if he thought he must give an answer, "His Royal Highness visited St. Petersburg. He was received very graciously, but he is quite certain the Russians want our country."

"Of course they do," the Duke agreed. "We all know that. It has been difficult for Her Majesty to help him until now."

"Very kind and very helpful. We are very grateful," the Baron replied.

"And is His Royal Highness pleased?" the Duke asked.

For a brief moment the Baron paused. Then he said, a little hastily, "Yes! Yes, he is very pleased. He admires the English very much, and English Brides are a big success in the Balkans."

The Duke only hoped that was the truth. He could not help feeling that if Alicia were to be shut away with the two dreary women who had been sent to escort her, she would undoubtedly be extremely bored and unhappy. The only consolation he could see was that if, as he suspected, His Royal Highness was looking for amusement elsewhere, Alicia would be able to come home and spend at least part of the year in England. However, he was too tactful to say this aloud. He merely talked of what arrangements were being made for the Wedding, which, as far as he could make out, was to be a show of strength to the Russians.

Fortunately, the Baron and his wife did not wish to stay long. They had an invitation to a tea party with a Member of the Cabinet, and another to a special dinner which was being given for them tonight by the Prime Minister. They drove off after thanking the Duke profusely and begging him and his daughter to be ready to leave for Rasgrad as soon as possible.

The Duke gave a sigh of relief. Before Alicia could say anything, he said, "All I hope, Dearest, is that the rest of his countrymen are not such crashing bores as their Secretary of State for Foreign Affairs."

"I cannot do it, Papa. I cannot!" Alicia said. "I cannot be with people like that for the rest of my life. How could I?"

"I think," the Duke said slowly, "from what I have learned from the Baron, you will be able to spend a great deal more time in England than we anticipated."

"Why should you think that?" Alicia asked in a dull voice. Her Father told her what the Baron had said about the Prince enjoying himself.

For a moment she brightened up. "That means I can come home while he is gadding about in Paris or somewhere like that," she said. "It certainly sounds better than I had hoped."

"I am almost certain of one thing," the Duke said. "He had no hand in arranging those dull women and that overtalkative man who represents Rasgrad."

"When I took them round the Picture Gallery, they talked to each other in their own language and were actually not interested in the pictures but, from what I gathered, how rich you were," Alicia said.

The Duke laughed. "That is what I might have expected from those dreary women, so let us forget them. After all, my Dearest, you will be a reigning Princess and will be able to invite whom you like to the Palace."

"The difficulty will be to find people I like,"

Alicia answered. "You know as well as I do, Papa, that most people who have any sense, unless of course they are Politicians, have no wish to be with Royalty because inevitably they are very dull."

The Duke knew this was more or less true, but he merely said, "The Prince is a young man. I cannot believe that his Palace is full to bursting with the three examples of Rasgrad that we have just seen."

"If it is, I am coming home immediately," Alicia said.

The Duke put his arm round her. "My Dearest," he said. "You must not talk like that!" Alicia looked up at him. "You know as well as I do," he continued, "that you are only being sacrificed because it is of great importance to this country that the Russians do not conquer any more Principalities than they have already."

"You told me the other night," Alicia replied, "that they have their eyes on India and that the young Cossacks are advancing at a tremendous rate towards it."

"Well, what happens in Asia will not affect you," the Duke said. "All you have to do, my Dear, is make Rasgrad as European as possible." He smiled at her as he went on, "As you know, I have some delightful friends in almost every country who I know will be only too pleased to receive an invitation from you."

There was silence for a moment, then Alicia said, "You do not think the Prince will expect me to sit at home with my knitting while he goes gallivanting with the Beauties of every country?"

The Duke, aware that the Prince was doing that already, had no intention of telling his daughter so. "I would not mind betting a large sum of money," he said aloud, "that when he sees you he will want to stay at home."

"I will not want him to do that if he is anything like the Baron," Alicia said. "He not only *looks* boring but he *is* boring."

The Duke laughed and replied, "If you say that sort of thing in Court it will not be received with a burst of applause."

"I never met three more dull or unattractive people," Alicia said. "I am frightened that if I stay long in their country I will grow like them."

"I am quite certain they are just a bad advertisement," the Duke answered. "I have some friends in the Balkans, as you know. I always thought the men were tall and handsome, and the women very attractive."

"If our visitors are an example of what the

Balkans can produce, all I can say," Alicia retorted, "is that you have been deceived."

Her Father laughed. "Forget them," he said. "I suppose I ought to send you shopping."

"If you think I am going to hurry in getting my trousseau, which I imagine few people will have a chance to admire, then I am not," Alicia answered. "I want a Wedding Dress and a great many other clothes. It will undoubtedly take a long time to choose them." She spoke positively but she had not calculated on Her Majesty the Queen and the Prime Minister having something to say in the matter.

The Queen sent a letter to the Duke saying that she thought they should leave for Rasgrad in two weeks time at the very latest. The Prime Minister confirmed this when the Duke went to see him.

"What is all the hurry?" the Duke asked.

"We have received a certain amount of secret information," the Prime Minister replied, "that the Russians are moving quite a number of their troops towards Rasgrad."

The Duke stared at him.

"They can hardly intend to invade the country if it is announced the Prince is taking an English Bride."

"For some reason I think it may concern His

Royal Highness himself," the Prime Minister replied. "They have not yet announced the engagement, even though I am aware that the Baron sent a cable to Rasgrad immediately when you agreed to the marriage."

"Then what is preventing them from doing so?" the Duke enquired.

The Prime Minister made an expressive gesture with his hands. "I imagine, although, of course, I should not say so except to you, that His Royal Highness has no wish to be tied to a woman's apron strings."

The Duke sighed. "Why did you have to embroil my daughter in this? She is very young and very beautiful. I think sooner or later she would have fallen in love with someone I would welcome as a son-in-law and with whom she would be very happy."

"I know what you are feeling," the Prime Minister replied, "but she really was the very last drop of Royal blood available. I looked through the archives myself and had several of my staff doing the same thing."

"Apparently, although my Mother was a Princess, her Family was not an important one," the Duke said. "But I do not know why you could not find someone else who would perhaps enjoy sitting on the Throne—my daughter is horrified at the idea."

"Of course, I can understand what the poor child is feeling," the Prime Minister answered. "But as you have doubtless been told a thousand times, England must come first."

"I know! I know!" the Duke muttered. "But it is very hard. If the people who were sent to represent Rasgrad are anything to go by, I can only think my daughter will die of boredom."

"I cannot believe that the rest of the country does not provide more amusing and interesting people than those three," the Prime Minister said. "I wish I could give you a firsthand description of Rasgrad, but, as you know, I have never been there."

"Nor have I," the Duke retorted, "and I have no wish to go now."

There was silence for a moment, then the Prime Minister said, "I think we are letting our imaginations run away with us."

"In what way?" the Duke asked.

"To begin with," the Prime Minister answered, "the Prince is young and I believe very handsome. If he has had experience with women, which he undoubtedly has, he cannot fail to appreciate your daughter's beauty."

The Duke could not argue with this statement. The Prime Minister went on, "When I saw her the other night, I was astonished at how beautiful she is and thought, like you, her Bridegroom must be worthy of her."

"I can only pray that he is," the Duke said. "Quite frankly, I think it would have been good manners and certainly more encouraging if he had come himself to look for a wife rather than merely relying on Her Majesty to do it for him."

"You are quite right!" the Prime Minister exclaimed. "But we cannot expect people always to do what we expect of them. If you ask me, I expect His Royal Highness is enjoying his last weeks of freedom."

"Weeks!" the Duke exclaimed.

"Remember, Her Majesty said you must leave two weeks from now," the Prime Minister stated.

"My daughter does not like that," the Duke remarked.

The Prime Minister shrugged his shoulders. "If you are brave enough to battle with the Queen over it, I am not. As you know, she always gets her own way."

"I am not prepared to battle with anyone," the Duke retorted. "All I want is my daughter's happiness and, at the moment, there is not very much in sight."

When he got home, the Duke had to tell Alicia that they would be unable to postpone leaving in two weeks' time.

"But I will not have all my clothes ready by then," Alicia protested. "I have chosen a fascinating Wedding Dress, but it has to be embroidered. I am sure it will take far longer than that."

"Then you will just have to be married in what you stand up in," her Father said. For a moment, the Duke thought she was going to be angry. Then she laughed.

"Can you imagine how disgusted they would be if I went in rags and tatters and said it was because the Queen insisted I should go to Rasgrad without waiting for my trousseau and, therefore, I came just as I was?"

"It would certainly be rather disconcerting," the Duke replied. "At the same time, my Dearest, you would still look lovely."

"You may think so, Papa, but would the Prince? He may, for all I know, have a passion for dark-haired Frenchwomen." She paused for a moment and shook her head. "In which case he is not going to admire my pink-and-white complexion and forget-me-not eyes."

The Duke laughed. "I think there is one thing of which we can be quite certain, and that is that His Royal Highness will admire you. And from what we have seen of Rasgrad so far, he is very lucky to have such a beautiful wife."

Alicia got up and put her arms round her Father's neck. "I want to stay at home with you, Papa. We have been so happy riding at home, arranging races with the neighborhood and hunting in the winter, which I have enjoyed as much as you."

"I know! I know!" the Duke exclaimed. "What you have to do, Dearest, is make your Palace as happy as you made the Priory."

"Well, I cannot make it happy without you and the people I have always loved and who love me there."

"They will love you when they see you," the Duke answered reassuringly, "and that is not a prophecy but a promise."

"I only hope you are right," Alicia murmured as she turned away from him.

The Duke arranged to travel to Dover, where the Baron and his wife would be waiting for them, in two weeks to the day.

"We must have one last long ride the day before we go," Alicia said, "and I do not want anyone else to be with us." She gave a little smile before she added, "It is something I will remember when I am far away from you."

"We will do exactly what you want, my Dearest," her Father replied, "and we will take our fastest and best horses."

The horses were waiting for them when they finished breakfast and rode off. It was a fine day, but had little sunshine.

As they galloped across the fields, Alicia felt, for the moment, that she was free of all her problems.

She was just happy to be with her Father.

Because she wanted to have a look at the whole Priory Estate, they stopped for luncheon at the far end of it, at a small Hotel. The Proprietor was honored and delighted to have His Grace there as a guest. A private room was arranged and a bottle of wine was brought to them. The luncheon was the very best the Proprietor's wife could possibly procure. For the moment, Alicia forgot what was to happen tomorrow and was supremely happy just being with her Father.

They set off rather later than they had intended and returned a different way, where the hedges were higher and the ground somewhat stony.

Whether because of the combination of both or because the Duke was getting tired they would never know.

While Alicia jumped the hedge safely and with plenty of room to spare, her Father's horse failed to clear it. The horse threw him on the other side of the hedge and, slipping on the stones, rolled on top of him.

Alicia went for help. The Duke was in great pain but they managed to get him back to the Priory.

The local Doctor was sent for and found, to everyone's relief, that apart from a broken leg and severe bruising, there was no further damage.

"I am afraid, Your Grace," Dr. Timothy Price said, "you'll not be able to walk or ride for some time. But it's a miracle you're not more injured than you are."

"It may be a miracle," the Duke said, "but it's an extremely painful one."

"I know that," the Doctor agreed, "but you have just got to stay in bed until you are better. I'll get the best Surgeon I know to examine you tomorrow, but I don't think I've missed anything." The Duke had known the Doctor for years; he was undoubtedly the best in the County.

When Dr. Price left, Alicia said, "I have been so

worried about you, Papa, and, of course, I will not be going to London tomorrow."

"I am afraid you have to, my Dearest," the Duke replied rather weakly.

"Of course I will not!" Alicia cried.

With an effort, the Duke said firmly, "But you have to! All the arrangements have been made. You cannot, at the last moment, let them down when you know the Baron and Baroness will already have left for Dover."

"I cannot go and leave you, Papa," Alicia protested.

"I am in good hands, my Dearest," her Father answered, "and when this damn pain stops all I have to do is to get my leg right so that I can ride again."

"But I will not be with you," Alicia exclaimed, "to look after you as I ought to be doing!"

"I am sorry, my Dear," her Father said. "But you are too important not to be present at your own Wedding."

"They can hardly have it if I am not there."

"No, of course not," the Duke said. "But you know that the Baron has told me that every arrangement has been made for your reception when you arrive and for your Wedding to take place the following day." Alicia made a grimace but did not speak, so he went on, "You can imagine what a mess there will be if you are not there, especially as it is not you who are ill but I, fortunately."

"Not fortunately, as far as I am concerned," Alicia protested. "Suppose you get worse and I am not here?"

"I am not going to get worse, I am going to get better," the Duke replied. "And, as you know, Dr. Price is an exceedingly good man and is bringing in the top Surgeon in the County tomorrow."

"I will not go! I will not!" Alicia cried.

The Duke sighed and shut his eyes.

"It is a Royal Command," he murmured, "and there is nothing you nor I can do about it. Let me rest for a little while, then come and sit with me, my Dearest."

Alicia went away almost in tears. When she went to look at her Father later that day, he was sleeping peacefully. She knew when he awoke he would be in pain from when the horse had rolled on him. She was also aware that his leg was badly broken and it would take time for it to be back to normal.

"Promise me he will recover," she said to the Doctor when they were outside her Father's room. "You know what it will mean to Papa if he cannot ride."

"Of course he will get better, and of course he will ride again," Dr. Price answered. "It has been a shock to you, as well as to your Father. I promise you he will have the very best Surgeon available to treat him, and I will come to see him every day." He paused before he added, "I also have an excellent Nurse to look after him. She will come to him tonight."

There was nothing Alicia could say to that, but she still wanted to find some excuse to prevent leaving her Father. He, however, was determined she should not alter any of the plans. Finally, with only her Father's Secretary to accompany her, she reached London and took the train to Dover, where the Baron was to meet her.

She had found it impossible to say goodbye to her Father without shedding a few tears.

"Do not be unhappy, my Darling," he said tenderly. "I promise that as soon as I am well enough —and that, I am sure, will be quicker than the Doctors predict—I will come out to Rasgrad and be with you."

"You promise that, Papa?"

"I promise," her Father replied. "I assure you I will come even if I have to be carried there on a stretcher!"

Alicia laughed, as he meant her to do. "I cannot

imagine you doing that, Papa. But you must take care of yourself. And please, please come to me as soon as you can."

"I will do that," the Duke promised.

The Baron and his wife were deeply concerned when they heard what had happened.

"I have never known my Father to have an accident out riding before," Alicia said. "It was a terrible shock when it occurred."

"Everything is waiting for you in Rasgrad," the Baron said. "I think if you refuse to arrive when they expect you, it might do a great deal of harm."

"That is what my Father thought and he, therefore, insisted that I come with you, even though you can understand that I wanted to stay with him."

"Of course you did," the Baron said. "But His Grace is wise enough to know that if anything as important as a Royal Wedding is canceled, it might turn to real trouble."

"What do you mean by that?" Alicia asked.

"People would be disappointed, and those who are trying to cause trouble in our country would find it a very good opportunity to step in and make a question of old grievances and resentments of those in authority."

Alicia knew quite well what he was trying to say. She was, therefore, silent.

They crossed the Channel with two private cabins, one for Alicia and the other for the Baroness and the Countess. The Baron said he preferred to be up on deck to watch the sea as they crossed it.

In her own cabin Alicia lay down. She was thinking of her Father and knew he would be thinking of her. She prayed that somehow they would be together very quickly.

I miss you, Papa, she said to herself. *I am so miserable going away with these dull people to a country I have never even heard of.* She could not help a few tears rolling down her cheeks. Then she felt ashamed of herself for not being more self-controlled.

Because it was impossible to lie down and not think of her Father and feel unhappy, she got up and looked out the window.

She could see the sun shining on the sea. The sky looked a bright blue above it. Every time she saw beauty it had an effect on her. She knew that if Rasgrad was beautiful, she would undoubtedly enjoy that, if nothing else. At the same time, leaving home was upsetting and frightening.

How shall I ever cope by myself with no one to advise me and no one to talk to? she asked herself. She felt again as if she wanted to cry. She walked to the

93

mirror and looked at herself. It crossed her mind that because she was so pretty, as everyone told her, perhaps the Prince might fall in love with her. If he did that, then everything would be easier than she expected.

At the same time, she knew she was taking what every other woman knew was a tremendous risk. She was marrying a man who did not love her. Being married meant she would never find real love, the love she thought would one day be hers.

Because her Father and Mother had been so much in love with each other and had been so happy, she had always, at the back of her mind, thought it would happen to her. Her Mother had said to her once, "When you marry, Darling, marry someone like Papa. I have been so happy."

A dreamy look had come into her Mother's eyes as she went on, "He said he fell in love with me the moment he saw me, and I loved him the first time I danced with him."

She gave a little laugh before she said, "Of course, I did not realize it was love. I just knew he was the most handsome and exciting young man I had ever met and hoped he would ask me again." She paused for a moment and then said, "It is what I want for you, Darling."

It had always been at the back of Alicia's mind. She had hoped that one day a young man, as tall and handsome as her Father, would see her and fall in love. *And I will fall in love with him,* she thought. *We will be so happy and have lots and lots of children whom we will love, and who will love us.*

Now it was all a dream, a dream that would never come true. She knew, because it was her Duty, she would have to try to make this strange man, who was to be her husband and whom she had never even seen a photograph of, happy.

How can I make him happy? she asked herself almost angrily. *How can anyone be happy unless they find the love Mama talked about? The love which Papa gave her and which now can never, ever be mine.*

She was still feeling lonely when they reached Calais. They hurried aboard the train which was to take them to Paris. Their compartments were reserved for them, and they were shown to them by one of the most important Officers on duty.

"You have only to ask the attendant for anything you require, M'Lady," he said to Alicia, "and it shall be brought to you."

"You have been very kind," Alicia replied. "Thank you." She shook hands with him, which obviously surprised him. She wondered later if, as a Royal personage, she should have been content with him just giving a bow.

However, she was tired and depressed from her feelings on board ship. She, therefore, told the Baroness she was going to rest at once.

"My husband has arranged for us to have a special meal," the Baroness replied. "It is going to be brought to his compartment. I am sure you will feel better after the sea voyage if you have something to eat and drink."

Rather reluctantly, because Alicia thought they would think her disagreeable if she refused, she went to the Baron's compartment. They were served what she thought was an adequate but rather dull meal. However, there was champagne to drink. Although she seldom had anything alcoholic, she thought it would at least help her to sleep. The conversation was all about traveling, and how uncomfortable some of the journeys had been.

Alicia was thankful when she could retire to her own compartment. She sat down in a comfortable seat. She was hoping that her Father would not find the train journey too uncomfortable and that, perhaps, he would be able to come even sooner than she anticipated.

* * *

They had to change trains at Paris, boarding the sleeper which was going to Trieste at dinner-time that day. There was the usual fuss and palaver which happened at every Station when a train arrived. People were frightened of losing their luggage and were determined that the Porter must not overlook it in the Guard's van.

However, the Baron saw to all this. Alicia, the Baroness and the Countess merely watched him.

The next train was very comfortable and well upholstered, as an Express should be, and was much more agreeable than the one they had left behind. The Baron explained they would have to be on it for quite some time.

"I consider nothing more important than traveling in comfort," the Baroness interrupted. Alicia had to agree with her.

Soon Alicia was alone in her cabin, and her thoughts wandered.

She thought she would stay awake thinking, as she had done when they had crossed the Channel, and feeling even more unhappy. To her surprise, she fell asleep almost at once. She dreamt she was riding one of her favorite horses over the fields at home with her Father beside her.

Alicia was woken up when a Steward knocked on the door. When he came in, he brought her dinner on a tray. She thought it was very kind of the Baron to have ordered it. He was looking after her so well.

She had been told they had to change trains before they reached Trieste and take what the Baron called "the small line" towards Rasgrad.

"I only wish the *Orient Express* was ready," Alicia said. "I have read so much about it; it will certainly be very comfortable for anyone who rides in it."

"That is just what I say to my husband," the Baroness piped in. "In my opinion, the trains we have in Rasgrad are out of date and should all be replaced."

"I have heard that story before," the Baron said. "But you know as well I do, trains are very expensive and there are a great number of other, more important things."

They were quite comfortable on the Express, but they would have to change again to the train which would take them directly to Rasgrad.

The train set off and, as there was no corridor on it, she learned that one would have to get out at the Station to have a meal.

Alicia could not say she was really uncomfortable. She recalled Dover, where she hated saying goodbye to her Father's Secretary, whom she had known since she was a child. She wondered what would have happened if, at the very last moment, she had refused to embark on the ship which was to carry them to Calais and instead gone home. She wondered to herself whether the Baron would have kept her with him by force, or whether they would have washed their hands of her and gone on to Rasgrad to say she was impossible.

The Baroness had plenty to say when her husband was not speaking, but the Countess hardly said a word! When she did, it was difficult to understand what she said.

Alicia had, therefore, buried herself in the newspapers she had brought with her. Those they had bought at the Station were in French.

She had also brought with her a book on European History, which she had put into one of her handbags just before she left home. She had found it in the Library and thought it might tell her a little more about the Balkans than she knew already. As it was written only two or three years ago, it would be useful in finding out the names of the other Principalities and what sorts of Government the adjacent countries had.

She could not help wishing that Rasgrad had been on the sea. She had read that the Brides whom Queen Victoria had sent out to the Balkans had been able to travel on Battleships. She thought it would have been really exciting to be in one of the Ironclads, the very latest ships to be built in Great Britain. She understood they protected the Mediterranean and the Sea of Marmara.

I love being at sea, she thought. *I find trains a very poor substitute for ships.* She realized, however, that everything possible was being done for her comfort.

When they had arrived at Calais, three train carriages had been booked for their party. Then they had changed to a larger, more important train.

Actually, Alicia thought it was really a bore to have to change; they would be quite content to go on as they were. But the train from Paris had sleeping compartments. When they actually settled down it was nearly midnight. Tired and upset at leaving her Father, she fell asleep immediately.

She awoke to find herself passing through Austria. "We will, unfortunately, have to change again," the Baron had said last night. "But then we will be nearly home and there will be no more discomforts." They had breakfast at a Station and traveled on until there was luncheon at yet another Station.

Alicia found the countryside interesting at first.

But then she kept thinking of her Father and wished she was with him. She felt sure if he had been with her, he would have told her interesting stories about the people who had governed this or that part of Europe.

They would certainly have laughed together at the serious way in which the Baron, despite the fact that he was Secretary of State for Foreign Affairs, regarded their journey. He kept asking Alicia fussily if she was comfortable. He also made certain that at every stop they got out and had a spe cially reserved place for them where they could see what was available to eat. Alicia tried to talk to him because she thought it was polite, but he really only enjoyed talking himself and did not listen to what anyone else said.

The Baron's wife had obviously given up long ago, Alicia thought, at making an effort to converse with her. As she could not understand the Countess and the Countess could not understand her, there was really no point in being polite and attempting any sort of conversation with her.

Finally, they reached the Junction where they were to have their last change on their journey to Rasgrad. Alicia had, at each change so far, asked if her luggage was safe. She made sure it was put into the next train before they moved off. She thought, after all this fuss, it would be an anti-climax if she arrived at Rasgrad without her Wedding Dress and only what she stood up in.

Fortunately, however, a Courier met them at the Junction and he saw to the luggage. The Baron fussed over it, too, and made sure every piece was moved from their train to the next.

Finally, they arrived at what was not a particularly important Station. Alicia saw that quite a number of people already sat in the train, which was at a side platform waiting for them.

Now they were given a special Drawing Room which had been attached to the last carriage of the waiting train. As she had always wanted to travel in one, she was very interested. She had never seen one before, although she had read about them, especially the one which was made for Her Majesty Queen Victoria when she visited France.

This was not a large carriage but it consisted of what was called a "Drawing Room" with comfortable armchairs and a small bedroom for herself. There was also another small bedroom on the other side of the carriage. It seemed there were no accommodations for all three of the party; some would be obliged to sit up all night in the Drawing Room. It later transpired that the Baron, his wife and the Countess had agreed to make themselves comfortable in the Drawing Room. Extra blankets were provided for them.

Alicia, however, surveyed her own small bedroom with interest. She longed for her Father to be with her so that he could discuss the Drawing Room, which she knew was only provided for Royalty and very important Diplomats and Politicians. *I must write and tell him all about this,* she thought.

There was a Pantry, which was little more than a cupboard. A Steward arrived with glasses of champagne. He promised that at the next Station, which was not far, they would be given dinner.

"This is certainly traveling in comfort," Alicia said to the Baron.

"It is how I always travel when I have the chance," he replied. "But this is especially provided for you, Lady Frederika. I am glad you are pleased with it."

"Very pleased, indeed," Alicia said. "I will write to tell Papa what he is missing. I am sure he will be sorry he is not with us."

"I am sure he will soon join us," the Baron said.

The train had still not moved. Having sipped a little champagne, Alicia went to the window to see what was happening on the platform. To her surprise, she saw quite a number of people arriving and thought they looked English, although she could not be certain of it.

It was getting dark but Alicia could see the women were somewhat gaudily dressed. There was a man who seemed to be in charge of them, hurrying along the platform. She thought, as there seemed such a fuss, that their connection had obviously come in late. That was why this train had waited for them.

Now, as they started to climb into the carriage to which the Drawing Room was attached, she could hear them talking and realized they *were* English. The man who was in charge kept hurrying them onto the train. The Station Master was talking to him.

I wonder who they are, Alicia thought. *As they are English people, perhaps I will get a chance to talk to them.* Just saying that made her long to be back home with her Father and not be afraid of what was waiting ahead for her. *If only I could turn the train around and go back the other way,* she thought. *Instead, I must go on to marry a man who, I am quite sure, has no wish to marry me, any more than I wish to marry him.*

She suddenly felt a sense of panic sweep over

her and wanted to run out and find a train to take her back home.

At that moment, the last person was hurried into the next carriage. The Station Master, who was escorting the group, blew his whistle. The train began to move; Alicia knew that even if she tried to get out, it would be impossible for her to do so.

It was soon dark, so she could not see what the countryside was like. There were a few stars coming out in the sky. But as the train traveled faster and faster, it was impossible to see anything.

Alicia sat down in one of the comfortable chairs and realized the Countess had tucked a blanket around herself. Having taken off her hat, she shut her eyes. *I wonder if she will wake up for dinner,* Alicia thought.

Then, almost as if Alicia had asked the question aloud, the Baron said, "I have just been told that, as we are so late in leaving, we will not be stopping for dinner as planned. We have to make do with sandwiches which have been left in the Pantry. I think there are also some very pretty cakes."

"I do not think we will be hungry," Alicia said, to be polite. "I expect it was those English people who held up the train."

The Baron nodded. "Yes, you are right," he

said. "They are English and they are going to perform at the Palace, as well as in town."

"Perform?" Alicia questioned. "What do they
do?"

"I was told they put on one of the most successful shows in London," the Baron told her. "Now
let me see! I heard the name! The man who does it
is Bill Bellow, and he calls his show in London
'Bellow's Belles.' "

"What do they do?" Alicia asked again.

"I think they sing and dance, and all the performers are very professional. In fact, His Royal
Highness saw them in France and particularly
wanted them to come to Rasgrad." He paused,
then added, "I suppose that the Prince has issued
his invitation to concur with the Wedding, when,
of course, everyone will want to be entertained."

Alicia was interested. She wished she had been
able to find out when she was in London what was
successful in the Theatres. But because she had
been asked to so many parties and also had to do
so much shopping, she had not been able to attend
the Theatre as she had wanted to do.

"But what do the Beauties do, exactly," she enquired, "except look beautiful?"

The Baron laughed. "I am sure they think that

is enough. But I believe they sing and dance brilliantly, and there is a man, I am told, who plays piano very well. But I do not know more." He smiled before he added, "But, of course, you will see them when you arrive at the Palace, and I expect they will give a special performance for His Royal Highness and yourself."

"I hope so," Alicia said. "When we stop at the next Station, I will look to see if the women are real Beauties."

"Unfortunately, as you just heard, we are not stopping until we arrive at Selkiz, which is the Capital," the Baron said.

"Oh, I had forgotten," Alicia answered. "That is why we have our food with us."

"Which now I will go and get for you," the Baron said. Alicia would have offered to help him, but he made it quite clear she should stay where she was while they waited on her.

After a meal of rather thick sandwiches and a little more champagne, she felt tired and went off to bed. The rest of the party still had a great deal of food left to eat, as well as champagne to finish off. The Baroness, sitting next to her husband, still had quite a lot to say to him.

No one wants me, Alicia thought, *so the sooner I go*

to sleep the better. She undressed but thought she might be cold, so she put on a pretty dressing gown over her nightgown.

Then she shut her eyes and started to say her prayers. She was asking God for help so that things might not be quite as bad as she expected.

Suddenly there was a resounding crash, and Alicia knew no more.

4

The crash came from behind Alicia.

Before she could move or get out of bed to see what had happened, another crash brought the ceiling down on her head, and she fell back unconscious.

The train came to a standstill but there were still more crashes. It was difficult, as it was now dark, for anyone to see what had happened.

Not until the following day was it learned that the train in which Alicia was traveling was almost three-quarters of an hour late in starting. The other trains along the line had not been notified.

The train on which Alicia was traveling had caught up with a freight train. As her train was going very fast to make up for lost time, it smashed into the freight train before either train was aware of the other. As it did so, another train, also traveling very fast, came up from behind and crashed into the Drawing Room of the train on which Alicia was traveling.

The pandemonium in the dark, from the people who were alive, was noisy and terrifying, even to those who were not injured.

The only man who kept his head and began giving orders immediately was Mr. Bellow. He was terrified that his performers had been injured. Bill Bellow had been on the stage since he was a boy. He had, at first, been with traveling performers who moved about the countryside giving shows in small towns. Because he was very talented as a magician, a singer and a dancer, he gradually found his way to London. He was a great success in the smaller Theatres.

Mr. Bellow was nearly forty years of age when he decided to start his own show. He had accumulated an enormous amount of experience from the other performers with whom he had traveled and acted in London. He realized that in most places where he went, the women were not very attractive. He, therefore, thought up the idea of "Bellow's Belles." He chose six of the most attractive and talented young women he could find. They danced and they sang, and from the moment they appeared, they were applauded by every man in the neighborhood.

With them were six men, including himself, a Pianist, a Violinist and a Drummer and two young Comedians, who were also very good dancers.

When the women had done enough performing, they turned somersaults to the delight of any children watching the show. There was no doubt that "Bellow's Belles" were a success in England. He, very bravely, tried them out on the Continent. There was no doubt, they were a greater success in Paris than they had been elsewhere.

It was where Prince Lintz of Rasgrad first saw them. He was delighted with the beauty of the women Bellow had chosen.

Mr. Bellow had been wise enough to make certain they would be a success on the Continent by being fair-haired and blue-eyed. They were also intelligent enough to try to learn a little of the language where they performed.

As they found French easier than any other language, Bellow took them on a tour of France, ending up in Paris. And it was in Paris where they shone brilliantly. They were written up in Parisienne newspapers as *"one of the most amusing shows England has ever sent us."*

The Prince was entranced with the fair-haired Beauties who, under Bellow's teaching, were extremely efficient at everything they did. They were so beautifully dressed that the women admired them almost as much as the men did.

It was when he was leaving Paris and had spent a very amusing evening with one of the Beauties that the Prince suddenly thought of inviting them to Rasgrad. He was sure they would be a huge success in the Capital. He even went so far as to ask them to stay at the Palace while they were performing.

Actually, he had his own Theatre which had been built by his Grandfather after a visit to Russia. His Grandfather had been extremely impressed by the private Theatres the Russians had built in a number of their Palaces.

As it happened, the Prince had never bothered very much about his Theatre. It was kept for a performance of the village children at Christmas when they did the Nativity play. It was also used for Prize Giving for certain of the Schools of which the Prince was one of the Patrons.

He had already been told before he left for Paris that every effort was to be made on his behalf for him to have an English Bride. He was, at first, horrified at the idea of having to marry any woman, unless he particularly wanted her as his wife. But he was persuaded by the Prime Minister and

Members of the Cabinet that this was the only way for the country to have real protection from the Russians.

They were infiltrating every part of the Balkans, and, therefore, he must be supported by the British. Because he was devoted to his country, he was aware, like all Princes of the Principalities, that the Russian menace was very real. He, therefore, finally agreed to allow his Secretary of State for Foreign Affairs to go to England, with orders to beseech Queen Victoria to send Rasgrad an English Bride.

The Prince was depressed at the thought. At the same time, when he saw "Bellow's Belles" in Paris, he realized how very attractive Englishwomen could be.

He then decided "Bellow's Belles" would grace his Wedding by giving performances, as they were undoubtedly the most beautiful women he had ever encountered. He did wonder if his Bride would resent the performance of "Bellow's Belles" if she were not as beautiful as they were.

Because he had traveled a great deal and spent some time in England, he had thought the average English girl of the age he was obliged to marry would be rather stupid and not particularly well dressed. But he had seen women on the stage and at parties who were outstandingly beautiful and were, of course, fair-haired and blue-eyed.

But to find six of them all together in one piece, so to speak, was something that amused, intrigued and inspired him not to lose sight of them. He had, in fact, begged Bellow to bring his Company to Rasgrad. He had offered to pay not only their expenses but a very large amount for their performance, which bribed Bellow into agreeing.

"You can easily, when you leave me, go into Austria, which is next door," he said. "I am sure they will appreciate your girls there, as they pride themselves on having the most beautiful females in the whole of Europe."

Bellow was rather intrigued with the idea. He also thought he had stayed long enough in Paris. He had grown used to traveling and, success or no success, he wanted to try new places because they interested him. Because his performers were so attractive, not only to look at but in what they did, he was always richer, never poorer, anywhere he stayed.

What really annoyed him, more than anything else, was when his women were such a success that they were taken away from him. For instance, one girl, who was not only exceedingly beautiful but an outstanding dancer, was lured away in England by a rich young man. Finally, because she still hesitated as to whether to leave her very comfortable job to be his mistress, he offered her marriage. That was something she had no wish to refuse.

Bellow, therefore, had to find someone else to take her place. It had not been easy. He had interviewed nearly a hundred women before he finally found one called Annie. She could dance and sing, almost as well as the one he had lost. It was this episode which had persuaded him that he must travel abroad. He had never regretted it.

Of course, some of his girls, as he called them, became mistresses of rich men who found them irresistible. The lonely men would pay anything if they could spend their free time with them. But because "Bellow's Belles" were continually moving, Bellow did not lose as many of his girls as he might have.

It was in Paris, where they were performing for the second time, that Prince Lintz saw them.

They had received a great deal of complimentary publicity in the newspapers. At the same time, the Frenchmen, with their flattering compliments and their flirtatious ways, made Bellow frightened of losing some of his Beauties. This was another reason why he accepted the Prince's invitation, although he had never gone so far away from home before.

Nevertheless, the years he had spent traveling had taught him a great deal about leadership. So, the moment the train crash echoed and reechoed through the darkness outside, he realized he had to act quickly if he was to save his performers.

Already, where the trains had run into each other, there was a flickering of flames. He knew those who had been injured must be taken out of the carriages immediately. It was, therefore, he who gave orders, rather than the Guards of the train, who seemed as bewildered and unable to cope with the situation as the passengers.

To every man who was standing on his feet, Bill Bellow gave the order to get people out of the train. As they had been passing through the countryside, there were grassy fields on either side of them. This meant there was no difficulty in lifting those who were hurt out of the train and onto the grass.

Fortunately, none of the men in Bill Bellow's Company were badly wounded, although one man had a cut on his forehead and another had injured his leg.

As the girls were lifted out, most of them were crying or shaking with fright. But on Bill's instructions, they started to work on another part of the train.

Toward the front of the train, some of the passengers were shouting from the windows. Others had climbed out to ask what had happened. Actually, comparatively little damage had been done to the front of the train, but the impact had driven the engine of the train in which Bellow was traveling partly off the lines. Fortunately, there was not a great number of people in Bellow's part of the train.

The Drawing Room at the end had been crushed completely by the engine, which had smashed into it in the darkness at great speed. Alicia, in the front part of the Drawing Room in the Sleeping carriage, had been hit heavily on the head by something falling from the ceiling and had no idea that anything was happening. Two of Bellow's men lifted her out of the bed and put her down on the grass. They covered her with a blanket and, when Bellow called them to help with the other carriages, left her unconscious on the grass.

The men from the other trains now began to get busy. Soon it was discovered that the three people sitting in the Drawing Room had all been killed.

Shortly, Bellow realized that people living in the vicinity were arriving to find out what had happened. The Farmer who owned the land where the catastrophe had taken place was saying very loudly and clearly that he would not be responsible for such a mess on his land. He had always said that allowing trains to run through it had been a mistake. But no one wanted to listen to him. In fact, as most of the locals were employed by him, they moved away as soon as possible, realizing their Master was not at his best when he was extremely annoyed.

Fortunately, although the man was a Bavarian, he spoke a little French, so Bill Bellow managed to tell him that his troupe was wanted at the Palace. After the Farmer first pooh-poohed the idea, Bill Bellow convinced him to bring out his largest wagon to convey Bill Bellow's party to the Palace, which was only five miles away in the Capital of Rasgrad.

His wagon turned out to be even better than they had expected. It was meant to carry cattle to market, making it large enough for them to carry the piano and the drum, which were in the train's luggage van.

Fortunately this was close to the carriages where Bill Bellow and the Beauties had been seated with their rugs and blankets. These were piled into the wagon.

It was rather difficult to see, as it was a dark night. Although one or two of the men were carrying lanterns, the majority had to grope their way. In a few carriages, the lights had remained on, but in others they had been smashed by the impact.

"There's one girl missing!" Bill Bellow said.

"I expect it's Annie, who'd gone to bed," one of the girls said in response.

"I'll find her," one of the men said. "Perhaps she's slept through it."

"More likely she's unconscious," another girl remarked. "I wish I was."

"Oh, you're all right, Katy," someone answered. "You always complain more than anyone else."

"Am I likely not to, in this mess?" Katy said. "I wish we'd stayed in Paris."

"I think it was you," one of the girls replied, "who forced us away."

"Why do you say that?" Katy asked.

"Because you were flirting so much with that good-looking *Comte* that Bill Bellow got nervous you'd go off with him and we'd be without you!"

Katy laughed. "Well, I did think of it. But as he had a wife and three children, I rather thought it was just a short engagement, so to speak."

They all laughed at that.

Then two men came back carrying a large

mattress on which there was a girl, covered with a blanket.

"Oh, here's Annie," one of them said. "Put her in and then we can get off."

They moved so that Annie could be put on the floor of the wagon.

"She can't be sleeping, after what we've been through," Katy said.

"Unconscious more likely," another remarked. "It's what I was at first, if you want to know, and now I've got a terrible headache."

"Well, thank goodness we can go to the Palace!" Gertie exclaimed. "If nothing else, they should have comfortable beds—just what I want at the moment."

The men who had arrived to help were now looking rather dismally at the number of people lying on the grass. They had taken them out of their compartments, but the Farmer was thinking it was unnecessary and they might just as well have stayed inside the train. Regardless, it would be impossible for anyone to move them at the moment.

Bill Bellow's fear of fire had obviously been unfounded. But the trouble would be how the train, which had run into the Drawing Room, would ever be able to carry on. The Drawing Room itself, having fallen to the ground, would make it impossible for any train to move up the line for days, if not weeks.

There was an anxious consultation taking place at the engine of the last train. There was a great deal of speculation as to whether it could back away from the smashed Drawing Room and proceed back to the town from which it had come.

Bill Bellow, however, was content with the fact that he had managed to get from the Farmer the only large vehicle in the vicinity. The sooner he got to the Palace the better. Six of his girls were in the wagon, and he had collected their luggage.

A single piece of Alicia's luggage, which had been taken out and placed on the ground, was picked up by the men helping Bill Bellow and put with the luggage belonging to the other girls.

No one was aware that Annie, who had been looking out the window when the crash came, had been killed instantly and had fallen out some way back. She was now lying with a number of other bodies on the ground.

At last they shut the door of the wagon. Bill Bellow sat up in the front, next to the driver, and Brian, the Pianist joined him.

"We are lucky to get away as quickly as this," the Pianist said. "And you were very clever to get this wagon."

"It's only because our destination is a Royal one," Bill Bellow replied.

"They are all talking of having to wait until the morning," the Pianist said, "for the train people to come and cope with the damage."

"But I was thinking," Bill Bellow said, "that His Royal Highness will want us at the Palace and they will not accept any excuse."

The Pianist laughed. "It's a miracle we've got away as we have."

"Luckily, there's not been too much damage," Bill Bellow replied, "and the girls, after a good night's sleep, will be ready to get to work in the morning."

The Pianist laughed again. "All you think about is the performance," he said.

"It is why we are here and why I am who I am," Bill Bellow replied, "and don't you forget it!"

"I am not likely to," the Pianist retorted. "But I think, if you ask me, after this shock, the girls will want to have a rest, if nothing else."

"I expect I can arrange it," Bill Bellow said. "But you know what Royalty are like. Come hell or high water, they expect to have what they want and won't listen to any excuses."

"Well, I expect we'll do our best as we always do," the Pianist agreed, and shut his eyes because he was tired.

It took them quite some time to reach Selkiz, the Capital of Rasgrad.

The lights on the roads and in the windows were welcoming after the darkness of the country-side through which they had driven. The men had two lanterns in the front of the wagon, but they were of very little help at this time of night. There was no moon, and the stars produced only a very small amount of light.

Selkiz was not a large town but, as the Capital of the country, it contained a great number of people. Still, the streets were empty, and it took some time to find a man who could direct them to the Palace.

He did not understand their language nor did they understand his. But finally he pointed in what they hoped was the right direction and they drove off. When finally they saw the Palace, there was no doubt that they had come to the right place. The very large and impressive structure was set back, high above the City.

The sentries at the front gates told them to proceed round the side. By this time, the driver was tired and the two men sitting on the not-very-comfortable seat beside him were tired, too.

The sentries on duty at the next gate, realizing who they were, took them up to the Palace, and after a great deal of commotion a man was found who spoke English. He was actually there as a translator but had gone to bed, thinking that the party he was expecting from Paris must have missed the train and would doubtless arrive to-morrow.

He had been fetched out of bed and was exceedingly surprised to see the troupe at this time of night. When he heard there had been a train accident, he was perturbed, and sent another man to tell the Officer in Charge. However, Bill Bellow informed him that the Company was tired and should be taken to their bedrooms as soon as possible.

They were shown into comfortable rooms at the side of the Palace which were kept for servants and visitors who, if they were Royal, brought an Armed Guard. After the girls had quickly chosen which rooms they would have, the two men with the dancers carried in the mattress.

"Surely she's come round by now?" Bill Bellow asked as they waited at the top of the stairs for them. "I understood she was not badly injured but merely unconscious from the shock."

Alicia was lying sideways. Her long and golden hair had fallen over her face, and since the blanket was piled high up, it was impossible to see her clearly.

Bill Bellow, however, bent over and pulled back the blanket. "Come on, Annie," he said, "it's time to wake up."

The two men who had carried her upstairs went away with the translator to find what bedrooms they were in.

In the light from the lamp which had been placed near the mattress, Bill Bellow looked at the woman with astonishment: she was certainly not Annie. The girl, who was either sleeping or, more likely, unconscious, was far more beautiful than anyone else in his Company. In fact, she was so beautiful, he could only stare at her in sheer astonishment.

Then he bent forward and felt her pulse. Her skin was warm and her pulse was beating. She was obviously not dead. He wondered if someone so beautiful had perhaps been shocked into unconsciousness and was not reviving as quickly as someone less fragile would have done. He figured it would be best to see to her in the morning. He, therefore, put back the blanket, blew out the lights and left the room. It was too late, he thought, to ask questions. Only one thing was quite certain: one of his girls was missing and there was a stranger in her place.

I'll settle the whole thing in the morning, he thought, *and find out who she is. In the meantime it is best to say nothing.*

He thanked the man who had shown them to their rooms and told the Pianist and the other men he was going to bed.

"At least we are all here," one of them said, "and judging by the number of people who have been knocked out, we have been lucky."

"Were there many?" Bill Bellow asked.

"I saw three crumpled bodies in that Drawing Room at the back of the train," the man answered. "I saw them coming aboard at the Station and thought, as they were shown on by the Station Master, they must be of some importance."

"I noticed *them,*" Bill Bellow said. He thought as he went to his own room the least said about it the better.

The girl who had replaced Annie—who he was certain was dead—was certainly one of the most beautiful young women he had ever seen. *If she cannot dance and she cannot sing,* he told himself, *at least the people can look at her.*

Then he told himself there was no reason to think that she would wish to be employed by him. If she were an ordinary person on the train, as he suspected she might be, she would obviously want to return to her rightful place. Although it seemed unlikely that might be at the Palace itself.

Whichever way it is, I suppose I'll have to look for another girl from somewhere, he told himself. *But it's not going to be easy in this part of the world where most of the women, as far as I know, have dark eyes and dark hair.*

He undressed and got into bed. Because he was tired, as was the rest of his Company, he fell asleep immediately.

In the morning, Alicia awoke and wondered where she was. She was in a strange room, one she could not remember ever having seen before. She could not think why she was there or what, in fact, had happened.

I must be dreaming, she told herself. *What am I doing in this place, and where am I?*

She was still sitting up in bed and looking round when there was a knock on the door. To her surprise, when she said, "Come in," a strange man entered. He was middle-aged, with what she thought was a kindly face. "Good morning!" he greeted her, coming towards the bed. "Are you feeling better?"

"I am wondering . . . why I . . . am . . . here," Alicia stammered. "What . . . happened?"

"There was an accident on the train," Bill Bellow said, "and I think you must have suffered a concussion, although you did not seem to be otherwise injured."

"On a train?" Alicia asked. "Why was I on a train?"

"I have no idea," Bill Bellow replied. "But you were put by mistake into the wagon which I had engaged for my guests. We came here, leaving everyone else in a terrible turmoil."

He saw she was looking puzzled and enquired. "Who were you with? I cannot imagine how you came to be with my party."

Alicia did not answer for a moment. Then she said, "I do not know why I was on the train and why I am here."

Bill Bellow sat down on the end of the bed. "Now listen, Dear," he said. "I know that you are suffering from a concussion. I have seen it before. Your memory will come back, although it may take a little time. Just think for a moment and tell me what your name is."

There was silence.

Then Alicia murmured, "I do not know!"

"Are you quite certain?" Bill Bellow asked. "Perhaps it's Betty, Gertie or Gwen."

He said the names slowly but realized that none of them meant anything to Alicia. "Now don't you worry! You've got a concussion; I suspect something hit you on the head."

Alicia put her hand up to her forehead. "It hurts me here," she said.

"You were hit by the ceiling, which came down in the carriage where you were asleep," Bill Bellow explained. "But don't worry, you'll remember everything in time."

"But where can I go, where can I stay?" Alicia asked.

"We are in the Palace of Prince Lintz of Rasgrad," he answered.

"I do not know him. I have never heard of him," Alicia said. "Why should he have me stay in his Palace?"

This was exactly what Bill Bellow wanted to hear. "Now listen to me," he said forcefully. "You've just got to rest and take things easy. Then you'll be able to tell me if you can sing or play the piano."

There was a pause for a moment.

Then Alicia murmured, "I think I can play the piano, but I know I can sing."

"Very well then," Bill Bellow agreed, "that's just what I want to know. In the meantime, just take things easy until you feel better."

"But I cannot stay here if I have not been invited," Alicia said.

"You are staying with me," Bill Bellow remarked. "I have here my girls who perform on the stage. Do you understand?"

Alicia nodded.

Then he went on, "What they really have to do is look beautiful. Just as you look. You are very beautiful, do you know that?"

"Am I?" Alicia asked weakly. "I do not think I remember what I look like."

"Well, you soon will when you look in the mirror," Bill Bellow commented. "In the meantime, I want you to stay here and have your breakfast, then I will come and talk to you. Perhaps you'll feel better by then."

She nodded meekly as he walked to the door.

"Now don't come out," he said, "until we know

a little more about you. I'll tell the others not to
disturb you."

He was gone before Alicia could ask him what
others and make sure he had really said she was in
a Palace.

Why should I be in a Palace? she asked herself. *I
have never been in a Palace and I do not want to be in
one.* She tried to think of her name. She thought if
she had a name she must have a Mother and a
Father. Although she tried, she could not imagine
what they looked like or who they were.

The strange man who had come and sat on her
bed had talked about a train. But she could not
remember a train. She put her hand up once again
to her forehead and realized it was very tender.

"He said something had hit me," she said. "I
wonder what it was." She could not think what had
happened. Then, because her head was hurting,
she lay down again on the bed. As she did so, she
realized she was wearing a nightgown.

"I cannot remember going to bed," she murmured. "I must have some other clothes."

She was still worrying about herself when the
door opened and a maid came in. She had her
breakfast on a tray and put it down on a small
table which was beside the bed.

"Thank you! Thank you very much," Alicia said, sitting up.

The maid smiled at her and said something in a language she did not understand. Then she went from the room, shutting the door behind her.

It is all very strange, Alicia thought.

At the same time, she was hungry. The breakfast was a warm croissant with honey besides something in a covered dish. She lifted the cover and saw there were sausages. They smelled delicious and she was very hungry, so she quickly ate her breakfast and poured herself a cup of coffee. She then felt better.

Now I will soon remember who I am and why I am here, she told herself when there was a knock on the door. When she said, "Come in!" in English, the same man who had talked to her before appeared.

"Are you feeling better?" he asked.

Alicia nodded. "Yes, I am better," she answered. "But I cannot remember how I got here."

"Never mind about that," he said. "I promise you, it will come back. I have known people who have had concussions before and it has sometimes taken a week or more for them to remember their names."

Alicia stared at him. "I do not remember my name!" she told him.

"Then what shall we call you?" Bill Bellow asked. "I try to find a nice name for my girls but they always prefer the names they were given at their Christening. But I don't suppose you remember that happening."

He had meant it to be a joke.

But Alicia explained solemnly, "No, I do not remember that."

"Very well," he said. "We'll just have to find a name for you until you remember your own."

He thought for a moment. Then he asked, "What about Venus? That's what you look like at this moment."

"Venus," Alicia said. "It is a pretty name."

"It's the Goddess of Love," Bill Bellow explained, "and you can be quite certain a lot of people will want to love you."

"Why should they want to love me?" Alicia enquired.

He thought it was safer not to go into detail and merely replied, "I'm certain it's something that'll happen. Now what we have to find out first of all is what you can do. My girls have to perform and you told me you can sing."

"If I can talk, I can sing," Alicia said.

"Then hurry up and dress. We will go to the Theatre and see if you are exaggerating."

Alicia looked round the room. "I have no clothes," she stipulated.

"How stupid of me!" Bill Bellow exclaimed. "One of the girls was saying at breakfast there was a trunk which did not belong to anyone, so I imagine it must be yours. I'll have it sent up to you."

"Thank you," Alicia replied. "You are very kind. I wish I could remember my name."

"Until it comes back to you, we'll call you Venus," he said.

She did not seem very impressed. He, therefore, went downstairs to tell one of the men to take her case up to her room. He had already asked all the girls if it had belonged to them, but they had refused it. Bill Bellow knew quite clearly it did not belong to him. All the things which he took with him, including the dresses which the girls wore on the stage, were heavily labeled. His name was also written on his trunk itself.

He looked at the case which had come with Alicia and knew it was a very expensive one. Doubtless her background was very different from his and the girls he employed. At the same time, he felt that this girl had fallen down like a gift from Heaven. It would be a great mistake to refuse what the Angels had sent him just when he was deploring the fact that one of them was lost.

Even if she does not sing, he thought, *she will look lovely. I am sure I can think of a reason why she should sit and look at the audience even if she can't perform in any way.*

At the same time, in the back of his mind he was hoping she would be able to sing. Annie had been a singer; the whole performance would be unbalanced if she could not take Annie's place. *I will keep my fingers crossed and hope that the manna from Heaven will drop on my head,* Bill Bellow said to himself.

Then the door opened and a man in very elaborate clothes came towards him. "Mr. Bill Bellow," he said, "I am the Lord Chamberlain and I have learned what has happened. I can only apologize that such a terrible thing should occur as soon as you entered our country."

He shook Bill Bellow's hand and went on, "I deeply regret that one of your young women is among the dead. She will be buried, unless, of course, you wish for her body to be sent home with the others who died in that appalling catastrophe last night."

"How many people were killed?" Bill Bellow asked.

"Twenty-three in all, and among them, to our

great regret, was the Secretary of State for Foreign Affairs, Baron Gavrion, his wife and a Lady who accompanied them, the Countess Udelana."

"That must be very sad for you," Bill Bellow said.

"Very sad indeed," the Lord Chamberlain replied. "Also missing, although we are not certain she was on that particular train, is a Lady of great distinction in England, who was to have married His Royal Highness."

"That indeed is disastrous," Bill Bellow agreed.

"She may not have been with the Secretary of State," the Lord Chamberlain continued. "We have only just written to find out if she did undertake the journey or perhaps met friends and stopped on the way."

The Lord Chamberlain was talking to himself rather than to Bill Bellow. He was obviously agitated, prompting Bill Bellow to say, "I'm sure you'll find her later on. In the meantime it would, of course, be a mistake for us to perform until the mourning for the dead is finished."

"I thought you would understand," the Lord Chamberlain said. "But please make yourself comfortable. I expect His Royal Highness will wish to see you later. At the moment, as you can imagine, he has a number of people wishing to talk to him about what has occurred."

"Yes, of course," Bill Bellow replied. He waited until the Lord Chamberlain had left before he went to look for the rest of his team.

It passed through his mind that the beautiful woman he had discovered upstairs might, in fact, be the someone they were looking for. He told himself it would be a great mistake to force her to make her association with the people in the Palace until they made quite certain the person they were looking for had been on the train. In fact, they would think it rather pushy and strange if he suggested that one of his girls was the Prince's Bride.

She must have been traveling alone, he told himself. *Or perhaps her Mother or whoever was with her are among the dead.*

He paused for a moment before he mused, "One thing, as far as she is concerned: she'll not be mourning those she can't remember, and she might be more useful to me."

As he went to look at the Theatre where he had sent the Pianist and the Drummer, he was whistling. Things were not as bad as they might have been.

5

The Prince was sitting at his writing desk when an Equerry informed him that the Councillor, who had gone to see the result of the train crash, was back.

"Oh, show him in!" the Prince commanded.

The man, who was elderly and who was important in the Palace, came to the door and bowed.

"Good morning!" the Prince said. "What is your news?"

"I am afraid it is rather serious, Your Royal Highness," the man replied.

"Why?" the Prince enquired.

"Because what happened in the chaos was that all the bodies, either dead or injured in the crash, were taken out as quickly as possible, because they were frightened of the fire spreading. It is now almost impossible to identify them."

The Prince looked at him. "You mean there is no sign of my Bride?"

"None at all, Your Royal Highness," the Councillor replied.

There was silence for a moment, then the Councillor went on, "I talked with the Police who are now there and, of course, with the Officer and some soldiers who were sent there by Your Royal Highness."

The Prince nodded as the Councillor went on, "There are over twenty people dead, and a number of them are unidentifiable." The Prince sighed but did not interrupt.

"Some have been very badly injured," the Councillor continued. "They are unconscious or have broken limbs and several have lost a great deal of blood. They are being taken to the Hospital."

The Prince made an exclamation but he did not say anything, so the Councillor went on, "Then there are people who apparently escaped from the wreckage and went off on their own to find assistance. Or perhaps they felt safer in the woods than on the line."

The Prince sighed again. He knew that when people panicked they were inclined to do anything.

"What was so tragic," the Councillor continued, "was that the Drawing Room which contained the Secretary of State for Foreign Affairs, his wife and the Countess caved in with the impact."

The Prince put his hand up to his forehead. "It certainly sounds a mess," he said.

"I am afraid it is, Your Royal Highness. It is almost impossible to find out if Lady Frederika was taken off after the Drawing Room collapsed, whether she was put with the dead, or perhaps she somehow escaped with some of the other people into the woods."

"You are quite certain she was not in the Drawing Room with the Secretary of State, his wife and, of course, the Countess?" the Prince asked.

"She might have been," the Councillor replied. "But if we had not known they were in the Drawing Room, it would have been difficult to recognize either the Secretary of State or his wife."

The Prince made a helpless gesture with his hands. He felt it was very embarrassing to have to send a cable to England to say that the Bride sent to him by Queen Victoria had been lost on the journey. At the same time, he wanted to be quite certain she was not among the dead or wounded.

"Have you been to the Hospital?" he asked.

"Two Hospitals are engaged in taking in the people. They started early this morning," the Councillor replied. "In fact, there is every reason to suppose that, if she were escaping from the wreckage, a kindly cottager might have offered her hospitality."

"That seems to me unlikely," the Prince said as he sat down again at his desk. Now he was tapping his pen up and down on the table.

"What am I to say?" he asked, almost as if he was speaking to himself rather than to the Councillor.

"I think, Your Royal Highness, it would be a great mistake to be hasty over this," he replied. "I only made a preliminary tour on Your Royal Highness's instructions." He paused for a moment before he went on, "I am sure we will be able to recognize a great number of people when the blood is taken from their faces and they have been properly treated."

"Surely they are getting on with it and the people are not still lying on the ground?" the Prince asked.

"Some are," the Councillor answered. "But, as Your Royal Highness can imagine, we had no idea that three trains would run into another. Two of them were packed with people, a number of whom were holidaying in Rasgrad."

"Which, of course, means they have come here from all parts of Europe," the Prince said.

There was silence before he went on, "I am very anxious to keep this as quiet as possible. If it is known that Lady Frederika, whom Queen Victoria sent to be my Bride, is missing, the Russians may hear of it." The Councillor was obviously aware of this. The Prince continued, "In which case, as you well know, they will think it a special gift from the Gods. They will make themselves as aggressive as they possibly can and their infiltration will increase immediately."

"I am aware of that, Your Royal Highness," the Councillor said. "What I have just told you will be kept entirely secret."

"That is just what I am thinking," the Prince agreed. "We will say nothing. It would be a great mistake for anyone to know that the Lady Frederika was on the train. After all, we did not publicize it, as we wanted her arrival to be a great surprise when she actually appeared."

"I remember those were Your Royal Highness's instructions," the Councillor said. "Of course, the Prime Minister was aware of it and you told me, but I do not think a great number of people outside the Palace will be aware that she was on that particular train."

"I told them to be very quiet when the news came through on the cable that the Duke would be unable to accompany his daughter," the Prince said. "In fact, as it was very vaguely written, I think, quite a number of those who saw the cable thought that since the Duke was unable to travel, his daughter would stay home with him."

"We can easily say that was the truth," the Councillor said. "The less talk about Lady Frederika, the less speculation there will be as to whether she is on her way or has not yet left England."

"I am sure you are right," the Prince said. "One thing I do not want is any trouble regarding my marriage."

"Of course, of course," the Councillor agreed. "That is very good thinking, Your Royal Highness! I think if Your Royal Highness expresses, as you have already done once, how grievous the catastrophe has been and how deeply you regret the death of the Secretary of State for Foreign Affairs, that will give them enough to talk about for the moment."

"I am sure it will," the Prince answered. "What is more, I think I should visit the Hospitals as soon as possible."

"You should also visit the scene of the accident," the Councillor said.

"I would naturally be interested to see that!" the Prince replied rather sharply. "At the same time, it is a tragedy that while we have never had such a thing occur before, it should happen now when I am strengthening the country by being married." He spoke so forcefully that the Councillor, thinking the conversation was taking an uncomfortable turn, moved towards the door.

"I will, of course, make out a report which will go to the newspapers," he said, "of Your Royal Highness's distress at the accident. I will play down, as much as possible, the actual tragedy and the deaths which have occurred."

"Yes, do that!" the Prince said. "You are always good at that sort of thing. But I am quite certain the Press already will have traveled out there to make as much of the crash as they can."

"There, we cannot stop them," the Councillor replied. "But I am sure a visit from Your Royal Highness will give them something more to talk about than the actual result of the crash."

"Very well," the Prince agreed. "Give the order for me to go there this afternoon with an escort and make it clear that our Hospitals are, as usual, doing a splendid job in helping those who are wounded." He paused for a moment before he added, "I will, of course, send a personal letter of regret to the relatives of all those who have actually been killed in the crash."

"I will see to it, Your Royal Highness," the Councillor said. He bowed from the doorway as he left the room.

The Prince put down his pen and put his hands up to his forehead. He had fought violently at first against the idea of having to marry someone who not only came from another country but was chosen for him by Queen Victoria.

He had, in fact, joked about the other Principalities that had pleaded for a Bride to wave a Union Jack, as the Prince had translated it to himself. At the same time, he had been obliged to accept the decision of his whole Cabinet, and a great number of other Notabilities, that the only way to preserve Rasgrad was to have the support of Great Britain.

At twenty-seven he was enjoying himself enormously, not only in his own country, but in France and other places that he visited. He found they provided men, especially Royal Princes, with the opportunity to mingle with their most beautiful and attractive women.

It was while he had been in France that he had seen "Bellow's Belles." He had been so fascinated by the beauty of the cast that he had attended every performance night after night, and also had given a special dinner for them when the final performance was over. It had been exceedingly gratifying to those concerned with the show. It was then, because he was leaving the next day, that he had asked, with what to him was an inspiration, if they would come to Rasgrad and be part of his Wedding celebrations.

He was quite certain that his English Bride, if he was to judge by the Englishwomen he had met so far, would be prim and proper. She would make very little conversation unless he was talking about her personally. As it happened, he had not met many Englishwomen on the one journey to London he had made when he was just twenty-one. But he had found talking with those few rather difficult.

The pomp at Windsor Castle had been a bore rather than an attraction. He had thought the Queen herself was terrifying.

The only thing he had really enjoyed had been

the racing, which was taking place at Ascot during his visit. But he had found the men in the Jockey Club not particularly interested in him or his country. He had, therefore, spent a great deal of time in Paris.

It was the Frenchwomen who had taught him the first rules of flirting, and he had become an extremely ardent and successful pupil. He had, however, thought it would be a compliment to his English Bride if one of the main entertainments during their Wedding was the English troupe "Bellow's Belles."

Now he wondered: if Lady Frederika were dead, would it be correct to send them away without giving a performance? Then, he told himself, if the audience consisted of only one person—himself—at least he would see "Bellow's Belles" before they left the country. He, therefore, sent a messenger to tell them to practice as much as they wished in the Theatre but, owing to the unexpected accident which had occurred on their arrival, they must understand why he could not, at the moment, give them an actual date for their performance.

"I will tell them what Your Royal Highness has said," the Equerry replied when the Prince had given him the order.

"Also say there are carriages at their disposal," the Prince said, "and tell them to see the City and any part of the country which amuses them. If they want to ride, there are horses in the Stables."

He did not know why he added the last instruction, except that he remembered how, when he was last in England, every man he talked to seemed to want to discuss horses rather than women. That, of course, was very different when he was in Paris.

The Equerry hurried away to obey his instructions.

The Prince then sent for his Officer in Charge of the Palace. "I must have an escort when I visit the scene of the crash," the Prince told him. "At the same time, I do not want to draw more attention to it than it already has."

"It's the worst accident we've ever had, Your Royal Highness," the Officer replied.

"I know that," the Prince said. "But it would be a great mistake for the Russians to use it to create trouble." He paused a moment before he continued, "Therefore, play down the tragedy as much as possible. My visit this afternoon must be a friendly one more than a notable expression of grief."

"I understand, Your Royal Highness," the Officer said.

The Prince looked at the clock on his writing table and saw there was an hour before luncheon. Because he had nothing particular to do, he thought he would go to the Theatre and see if Bill Bellow and, of course, his beautiful "Belles" were there.

The Theatre, which had been built by his Grandfather, was extremely attractive. The auditorium, which rose at the back, held about forty people.

It had two Royal boxes on either side of the stage. The boxes were carved and painted a soft blue and the seats of the comfortable chairs were the same color. The background for what appeared on the stage had been painted by a number of famous artists and was original and more exceptional than that any Theatre the Prince had ever visited.

As he came down the corridor, he could hear the music playing. There was a gaiety about it which he felt, after his dismal morning, was something he really needed. He, therefore, slipped in through the door, but instead of going forward to meet the performers and, of course, Bill Bellow, he sat down in one of the back seats, aware that no one had noticed his arrival.

There were three girls on the stage dancing in the abandoned but brilliant manner which Bill Bellow had created himself. As they twirled and twisted, the movement of their legs was in itself something unusual and very different from anything the Prince had ever seen before. They danced until finally they sank down in a low curtsy.

Bill Bellow, who was sitting at the side of the stage, walked to them and said, "That was excellent! Just remember, Betty, that you must kick a little higher. In fact, a good four or five inches higher, if you are to be as good as Gertie." Then he said, "Sit down. I am going to ask Venus to sing for us."

This was not a name the Prince had heard while he was in Paris. Then from the side of the Theatre where she had obviously been watching, the most beautiful woman he had ever seen walked out. She was certainly new because he would have remembered her if he had seen her in Paris.

Although all the "Belles" were undoubtedly outstanding, he thought this one really deserved the name Venus. In fact, he had an impulse to move

nearer than he was at the moment, to make certain
he was not being deceived.

On the stage there was what seemed to be a serious conversation going on. He did not move, but
bent forward hoping to hear what Bill Bellow was
saying.

"Have you thought of a song that you can sing
for us?" he asked.

"I have been trying to remember the one I
knew well," the girl called Venus replied. "But the
only one I can think of at the moment is:

Where the Bee sucks, there such I
In a cowslip's bell I lie.

and I hope someone will know the music for it."

"Of course they will," Bill Bellow said. "That's
right, isn't it, boys?" He went to the corner of the
stage where the small orchestra sat.

"I think I know that," Brian said, "although I've
never played it."

"Nor have I," the Violinist replied. "In fact, if
you ask me, it's been out of date for years."

"That's true," Bill Bellow said.

There was silence for a moment, then Venus
said, "I think I can remember the music if you let
me play it."

The Prince thought that Bill Bellow looked surprised when he said, "Of course. Have a try!"

The man who was sitting on the stool in front of the piano got up and Venus sat down. Her hair was gleaming in the light as she did so. The Prince thought he had never seen such lovely hair or, in fact, such a lovely woman. He was sure that her tresses were a wig. Perhaps when he saw her up close, she would not seem as exquisite as she was from this distance.

Alicia sat down at the piano. As her fingers touched the keys, she remembered playing a piano somewhere else, although where it was, she could not put a name to. Then she realized Mr. Bellow was waiting and everyone else was quiet. Slowly her fingers seemed to feel the keys as they must have done, she thought, somewhere else, although again she could not remember where.

Then she began to sing.

The Prince was entranced by the softness and the deepness of her voice, as the performers certainly were. Bill Bellow himself was struck dumb with the beauty of it. There was no doubt that her voice had a magical way of almost drawing a listener's heart from his body.

Because the song she sang was soft, gentle and

in fact, very old, there was complete and absolute silence as if everyone had stopped breathing until she finished.

Then Bill Bellow said, "Who taught you to sing like that?"

"I . . . cannot . . . remember," Alicia said. "But did . . . it sound . . . all right?"

"It was excellent," Bill Bellow said.

With difficulty, the Prince did not shout out that it was wonderful. It was quite the most wonderful voice he had ever heard.

"Now what I want you to do," Bill Bellow said, "is sing another song, if you have one. Or perhaps the same one again, and my Violinist will follow you. Is that so, Bert?"

"I hope so," Bert said. "But if you ask me, she's perfect doing it with her own accompaniment."

"I rather agree with you," Bill Bellow answered. "But perhaps an audience would find it rather dull, if they expect us to be active."

"Not when she sounds like that," Brian said. "You put her on and let her play and, if you ask me, the audience will find it something new but very much to their liking."

Because the Pianist was saying what the Prince was thinking, His Royal Highness wanted to applaud him but thought it would be a mistake. Yet what he really wanted to do was meet the singer and find out if she was as beautiful close as she appeared from the back of the auditorium. Because he did not want to disturb what was happening, he sat back quietly and did not move.

Once again, Alicia ran her fingers over the keys. Then she sang a bright little song which was whistled by errand boys in London and hummed in the streets of Yorkshire. Somehow she gave it a depth and feeling which had not been there originally. And while it certainly was not a song which would have been applauded at Drury Lane, there was something in her voice which was almost irresistible.

When she sang the chorus for the second time it was with difficulty that the Prince restrained himself from singing with her.

When her hands left the keys, she turned to look at Mr. Bellow and said, "That is all I can remember at the moment."

"It was brilliant and will make everyone who listens to it feel happier," he said.

"That's true!" Betty agreed. "You're a real professional, that's what you are."

"I wonder if that is true," Alicia murmured.

"I am quite certain it is," Bill Bellow said. "If some London Theatre's weeping because you've left them, we're very glad to have you. As one of my 'Belles,' the audience will undoubtedly keep you playing for them by encoring everything you can give them."

"That is not much at the moment," Alicia said. "I am sure I know other songs, but I still cannot remember the words."

"They'll be back," Mr. Bellow said. "In the meantime, I'm going to rehearse the five girls, and I want you to watch them and see if you can dance as they dance."

He pulled out a chair and put it on the other side of the stage. "Now sit there," he ordered, "and tell me when they've finished their dance if you can copy what they are doing. At least you can have a try."

Alicia did not answer as she sat down obediently in the chair.

It was as the Pianist was sitting down on the piano stool and the Violinist was picking up his violin that the Prince thought he could wait no longer. He got up and walked down the center of the auditorium.

It was Bill Bellow who saw him first. "Your Royal Highness!" he exclaimed.

"Yes, here I am," the Prince said, "and I am very delighted to see you."

He walked up onto the stage. As the girls curt-sied, he shook hands with Bill Bellow.

"It is nice to have you here," the Prince remarked, "and I am very thankful that you were not injured in the terrible train crash last night."

"We were very fortunate," Bill Bellow said quickly. "As it was obviously depressing for Your Royal Highness, we are hoping to cheer you up."

"Are you feeling well enough to give me a short performance tonight?" the Prince enquired. "I will quite understand if you would rather postpone it for a day or so."

"Of course not," Bill Bellow answered. "We'll be far better doing our stuff than sitting about think-ing of what happened."

"You will have only a small audience tonight," the Prince said. "But, of course, now I want to meet my old acquaintances from Paris." He walked towards Gertie as he spoke and said, "It is nice to see you again. I am thrilled you are here in my country."

"We're very grateful to be here safe and sound," Gertie replied.

Because he was frightened that she might add that one of their members was missing, Bill Bellow quickly intervened. He introduced Betty, whom the Prince already knew, then talked about the troupe's success in Paris.

When he had shaken hands with all the people he had met before, the Prince looked towards the newcomer, who was standing by her chair at the far end of the stage. "I think this is someone new, whom I have not met before," he said.

"Yes, indeed," Bill Bellow agreed. "Her name is Venus, for a very obvious reason. Since she was very shaken last night, she has a little trouble remembering her parts."

"I can understand that," the Prince said. He was, in fact, looking at Alicia in astonishment because she was even lovelier than she had seemed from a distance. He had never seen such perfect pink-and-white skin or such vivid blue eyes. They seemed to light up her whole face. And her hair was certainly not a wig. The flickering of gold in it when she moved was one of the most beautiful things he had seen in a woman.

"I hope you will enjoy being here," he said aloud. "And you must not let Bill Bellow make you work too hard. There is a carriage always at your disposal and, if any of you wish to ride, there are horses."

Alicia's eyes lit up. "Horses!" she exclaimed. "I

would love to ride. I am sure Your Royal Highness has very good horses."

"I like to think so," the Prince said, "and they have won a number of races, but only here. I have not yet been presumptive enough to take them to England."

"Can I really ride one?" Alicia asked.

"But of course," the Prince replied, "and I suggest you look at them in my Stables." He smiled down at her before he went on, "Tomorrow morning, unless you are made to work hard by Bill Bellow, you can ride on the Steppes behind the Palace, which I find extremely beautiful in the early morning."

"I would love to do that," Alicia said. "I will look forward to seeing Your Royal Highness's horses."

"How do you know so much about horses?" the Prince asked. He had a feeling that Bill Bellow had little time for attending Stables when he was engaged in looking for Theatres and Concert Halls where his people could perform. Then he realized that Alicia was having difficulty in remembering why she loved horses, yet she knew she did.

The Prince was wondering how he could see more of her and said, "Give me a short performance this evening, just for myself and one or two of my special guests. Then bring all of your party to supper afterwards."

"That's very kind of Your Royal Highness!" Bill Bellow exclaimed. "We deeply appreciate the privilege."

"You will, of course, pay for your supper when you give me one of your brilliant performances here at seven o'clock," the Prince said. He paused for a moment before he added, "As you are probably tired after your regrettable experience of yesterday, it need not last long. We will have supper at eight-thirty."

He deliberately made supper at that time for the simple reason he had learned of old: that it was a mistake, if one wanted to see a theatrical performance, to ask people to dinner first. They always ate and drank too much and were invariably late for the performance itself.

Even though the "Belles" would not start their performance before he arrived, he found it difficult to wait to see Venus again. What was more, he wanted to learn everything about her. She was certainly different from the other girls even though they were outstandingly beautiful. There was something about her which told him that, while the others were beautiful in their own way, she was exceptional.

Because Bill Bellow knew the way to behave where important people were concerned, he escorted the Prince to the door of the Theatre and bowed respectfully as he left.

"Seven o'clock, and I will be counting the hours," the Prince said as he walked away.

As Bill Bellow went back to the Theatre, Gertie said, "Well, the Goddess has certainly shown us her talents. But if you ask me, His Royal Highness will expect more of her than just a song!"

"I was thinking the same," Bill Bellow agreed. "But we haven't seen yet if she can dance."

Alicia laughed. "Not like the others," she said. "I think they are wonderful. I have only been able to dance in a Ballroom."

As she spoke a puzzled look came over her face. "Why did I remember that?" she asked. "And what Ballroom was it, and where?"

Walking away to the Palace, the Prince told himself that the newcomer to Bill Bellow's show was extraordinary. She was more beautiful than anyone he had ever seen on any stage.

Where did he find her? he asked himself.

As he walked towards his Dining Room, he wondered why she had been so vague about what she could do. Of course, she had been upset by what had happened yesterday. The rest of the cast were extremely lucky they had not been injured in any way. In fact, as he had learned this morning when he had asked after them, even their piano and other possessions had come to the Palace intact and not in any way damaged by the crash.

Bill Bellow was extremely lucky, the Prince thought to himself when he heard about the terrible destruction caused last night.

At the luncheon table, he had been told of one man in the City who had lost his wife and daughter. Another whom he knew well had his leg badly damaged.

"You must make a list," the Prince had said to one of his Equerries, "and I will write personally to anyone who is suffering from this collision. We must be careful that no one is forgotten."

"A list is already being made, Your Royal Highness," the Equerry replied. "But we are finding it difficult to recognize the people who were burned."

The Prince shuddered. "I do not want to talk about it," he said.

He was thinking it would have been an even worse tragedy if those beautiful women he had seen on the stage had lost their looks or been crippled by what had happened.

He was, of course, extremely sorry that the Secretary of State for Foreign Affairs had suffered.

At the same time, the Secretary had been extremely successful as a Diplomat, and he and his wife had lived a good part of their lives.

The beautiful girls presented by Bill Bellow were still very young. The Prince was sure the newcomer, who was quite rightly named after the Goddess of Love, was not more than nineteen or twenty. She was young enough to be unspoiled by the type of man who frequented the Stage Door and who made a young woman grow up very quickly.

The Prince had the feeling, although he could not explain it to himself, that Venus, as they called her, was completely innocent and unspoiled by the world outside.

6

It was a lovely day.

On his way to the scene of the disaster, the Prince was thinking how lucky he was to be alive. He loved his own country; it was a particularly beautiful one—with its high mountains, its deep rivers and many miles of open land which he hoped would never be built on.

He could understand why people wanted to sing when the sun was shining on the flowers in the fields. At the same time, sunshine made the snow beautiful when it shone on the white-capped mountains in the winter.

What he could not understand, however, was why there was no sign of Lady Frederika.

It was quite obvious she had not been in the Drawing Room with the Baron and his wife and the Countess, who was her Lady-in-Waiting.

He had received a cable saying that the Duke

was unable to come with her because he had been badly hurt while riding.

It suddenly occurred to the Prince that he had heard nothing further from England, meaning the Duke might be worse or, perhaps, had died. In which case Lady Frederika would, at the last moment, have canceled her journey to Rasgrad. The more he thought of it, the more he was convinced that this was what had happened.

It might have been impossible for the Baron to cable him that Lady Frederika was staying with her Father. He only hoped this was true.

Although he knew it was for the good of his country, he had no wish to marry. So he told himself, with a sense of relief, that for the moment he was too busy with other matters to pay attention to a Bride.

When he reached the wreckage of the three trains, it was even worse than he had expected it to be.

Because the freight train had caught fire, the train which had crashed into it was very badly damaged. He could understand why the list of those who had died was greater than it need have been.

He was met by the Officer in Charge who, when he had been sent for, had tried to make some form of identification of those who were dead or injured. However, as he explained to the Prince, it had been very dark.

"It was pitch black, Your Royal Highness, as there was no moon last night. Men just pulled people out of the trains and put them on the grass, regardless of whether they were alive, dead or merely stunned."

"I am sure it was a problem for you when you did arrive," the Prince said.

"I did my best, Your Royal Highness, to separate the dead from the living but it was not easy," explained the Officer.

He paused for a moment before he went on, "I have been told to tell Your Royal Highness as soon as you arrived that we have found the luggage of Lady Frederika Templeton."

The Prince stared at him. "The luggage!" he exclaimed.

"Yes, Your Royal Highness. There was so much that it had been placed in the luggage van rather than in the Drawing Room, as we expected."

He then added, "I am pleased to say it is completely intact and undamaged."

The Prince drew in his breath. This meant that despite his hopes, Lady Frederika had definitely been on the train. "You do not think," he said, "that you have failed to identify Her Ladyship either in the Hospital or in one of the houses made available for those who were injured?"

The Officer shook his head. "It is very difficult to be certain, Your Royal Highness, but I can absolutely stake my career that Her Ladyship was not amongst the dead."

"Then what about the wounded?" the Prince asked.

"They are mostly men, as there were very few women on the train at that hour. Those who are in the Hospital are nearly all middle-aged."

"You are quite certain that every body has been lifted from the three trains?" the Prince asked.

"I have inspected them myself, Your Royal Highness, and I promise you that unless they are under the train itself where a carriage has collapsed, everyone has been cleared out."

There was no point in the Prince questioning him further. So the Monarch went to the Hospital and talked to the people there. He also called at a number of houses where they had been kind enough to take in those who were wounded. Yet there was no one among the injured who was young and pretty, which the Prince had heard about Lady Frederika.

When he drove back, he could only think that her luggage had gone ahead when she decided to stay with her Father. That was why it had arrived without her.

He was, however, determined that everything should be kept as quiet as possible so that the Russians should not know there had been any delay of the Wedding.

Despite the fact he had tried to keep quiet about it, of course, the Ministers had talked. Already the people in the City were planning how they would celebrate their Ruler's Wedding.

It is impossible to keep anything secret for long, the Prince thought to himself.

He knew that sooner or later he would have to give an explanation as to why Lady Frederika was not with the Baron and Baroness. At the same time, if she had been on one of the trains, it would be cruel to communicate with her Father and tell him she was missing that her body could not be found.

I will give it a little more time, he thought to himself. *But I am sure that Lady Frederika pulled back at the last moment because her Father grew worse or perhaps died!*

When he arrived at the Palace, a number of

people wanted to see him after they had learned he visited the accident site. Some of them had relations who had not been accounted for.

Inevitably, there were also Reporters from the National newspapers who rushed forward, as the Prince's carriage drew up at the front door, and asked him what had happened. They had been annoyed that the Officer in Charge had forbidden them to interview the sufferers in the Hospital or to take photographs until they had permission from His Royal Highness.

"I am deeply distressed for those who lost their lives and for those whose relatives will be mourning them," the Prince said. "It is, however, a little too soon to be quite sure that we have a correct itinerary of everyone who was on board."

He paused for a moment before continuing, "Therefore, you will understand I do not want there to be an official list of those who have lost their lives until we are quite certain that everyone is correctly identified."

There was nothing the Press could say to this. Only one was brave enough to ask, "Were you not expecting a visitor to come from England with the Secretary of State for Foreign Affairs?"

"I am extremely distressed at losing the Secretary of State, who was, as you know, a personal friend of mine," the Prince replied. "I will be in touch with his Family as soon as they are informed of his tragic death."

As he finished speaking, he disappeared through the door of the Palace. No one was allowed to follow him. The Officer in Charge of the Palace was in the hall waiting for him. The Prince asked him to come into his private Sitting Room.

"Things are worse than I expected," the Prince said as he sat down at his writing desk. "Also, they have discovered the luggage of Lady Frederika."

"Her luggage!" the Officer exclaimed. "In which case she must have been with the Baron."

"Her Father was injured just before she was due to leave," the Prince replied, "so she may have stayed and sent her luggage ahead with the Baron's. Lady Frederika, therefore, may not have traveled with them."

"Yes, of course," the Officer agreed. "I had not thought of that."

"I told the Officer in Charge," the Prince said, "to have her luggage sent to the Palace and put into a room which you must lock and make certain no one pries."

"I will do that, Your Royal Highness," the Officer promised.

The Prince gave a deep sigh. "Now let us try to

enjoy ourselves, but no one must know we are trying to put aside our troubles at the moment."

The Officer looked at him. They were the same
age and had actually been at School together when
they were quite small.

The Prince later had gone to England and spent
two years at Oxford University, so he spoke very
good English. He had also insisted, when he had
known he would have to marry an Englishwoman
to save his country, that all the Officers and important officials in the Palace should "polish up their
English," as he put it. Because, like him, they were
very anxious to keep the Russians at bay, they
obeyed him.

This was another reason why he had been glad
that Bill Bellow and his "Belles" were coming to
the Palace.

"What we must do, Anton," he said to the Officer, "is to forget for a moment our troubles and
enjoy the 'Belles' I have brought you from Paris."

"As you can imagine, Your Royal Highness, we
are extremely eager to hear them perform," Anton
replied.

"Now whom can we invite who will keep their
mouths shut?" the Prince asked. "Because it will
not look right if I am enjoying the company of
beautiful women when my future wife is either

dead or perhaps mourning her Father's death in England."

The Officer thought for a moment. Then he named three young men who, like himself, had been at School with the Prince and two others who were great friends.

They also were engaged at the Palace, as Anton knew the Prince would not want anyone outside to be aware that "Bellow's Belles" had survived the train crash and were performing in the private Theatre.

The Prince agreed to his Officer's choice, only adding—because he thought it polite—the Lord Chamberlain. It was, however, with a little relief that he learned later that while Lord Chamberlain was exceedingly grateful to His Royal Highness for the invitation, the Lord had members of his Family arriving from the country that very evening. He had arranged a Family dinner party for them.

The Prince was aware they were coming because they anticipated the Royal Wedding would take place soon after Lady Frederika's arrival. As he had already informed the Lord Chamberlain that no one was to know that something might have happened to the Bride, it was better for Lord Chamberlain to be at home rather than joining in at the Palace.

That meant there would be a very small audience. But he knew it would be enjoyable because afterwards he would have a chance of meeting the beautiful addition to "Bellow's Belles" whom he had not previously met in Paris.

She is certainly an asset, he thought.

He wondered how Bill Bellow had been clever enough to get her.

They had been rehearsing all morning.

Because he found it so attractive, Bill Bellow had loved Venus, as he called her, singing the Shakespearean song which he was sure would be known by anyone who was well educated. Her second song was one he had heard in Paris. He had particularly liked it because it was such a perfect tune. When Bill Bellow had suggested to Venus she should try to learn it, she had surprised him by sitting down at the piano and playing it.

"That is the one," he said. "That is very clever of you."

"I remember it, but I cannot remember where I heard it," Venus replied.

"Never mind that," Bill Bellow said. "It means, 'I Love You.'"

She smiled at him. "I remember something else," she said. "It is *Je t'adore.*"

172

Then to his astonishment she sang it in French. "That is splendid!" he exclaimed. "I did not know you knew French."

"I did not remember it myself until now," she replied. "But when I heard the tune, the words came to me."

"As I know the Prince speaks French perfectly," Bill Bellow remarked, "you must sing it to him."

"It sounds prettier and more real in the language in which it was composed," Venus said. Then she gave a little cry. "I remember that, too,"

"You are getting along splendidly," Bill Bellow answered.

He was, in fact, secretly frightened that she might find herself to be a member of one of the important Families in Rasgrad. Or perhaps worse still the daughter of the French Ambassador. In which case she would be taken away from him. As he was sure she was going to be one of the most important assets of his "Belles," he did not wish to lose her.

"Don't worry yourself," he said soothingly. "You're doing splendidly, and your voice is lovely. I can't say more."

She smiled at him. "It is terrible to have a blank in one's head. As you can guess, it is still very sore on top where something must have hit me."

"Don't think about it," Bill Bellow retorted. "We're very happy to have you here. The girls all like you, the boys think you're beautiful and the one thing left to do is charm His Royal Highness."

The others, who were listening, laughed.

"That's the way he always talks to us," they said to Venus. "And, of course, we want to be a success, which we have been in every country we have visited so far."

"I want to go to Greece," one of the girls said, "and now Venus is with us I feel they'll be very appreciative of how clever we are."

"I think perhaps it'll be almost too clever to arrive in Greece with Venus," Bill Bellow replied. "At the same time, we can try it. We'll not have far to go from here. I'm sure if we get down to the sea, we can find a ship to take us to Athens."

"Oh, that'd be wonderful!" one of the girls exclaimed.

"I know I love the sea," Alicia said, "and I feel I want to dance on the waves."

"Well, I think your dancing is not as good as your singing," Bill Bellow remarked. "But if you want to dance, Bert will waltz with you. He's an expert on swinging girls round."

Bert seemed only too eager to try it, but Bill

Bellow said, "We'll leave that for another time. If we're going to be here until after His Royal Highness's Wedding, we'll have to think up a number of new things to please him. At the moment, I think two songs for Venus is quite enough, if we are having dinner early."

The men agreed to this while the girls went to decide which dresses they would wear.

"I think I only have one evening dress with me," Alicia said.

"Well, if it is as pretty as the one you're wearing at the moment," Bill Bellow replied, "that'll do for tonight because you'll not have to change."

He paused for a moment and then went on, "I'll put you at the end of the show singing *Je t'adore.'* You can all come on and curtsy to His Royal Highness in what you were previously wearing, so you need not change."

"I am glad about that," Alicia said, "because I have nothing to change into."

She thought, however, he was not listening and she turned again to the piano. She played softly while he was giving orders as to what they should do.

As she did so, she kept thinking, *I must remember! I must remember! I know this song, but where did I hear it? Why, when I am English, do I know French?*

There was no answer to her questions. Then they went off to their rooms to rest before the performance. The rooms provided were comfortable but rather small, and Alicia kept thinking that she should be in a bedroom which was bigger and which had a bigger bed. But that did not tell her where it was or why she was thinking it. She only knew that the bed was very small and the room itself somehow constricting. Then she tossed a little trying to think back through the darkness of her brain.

It was then that one of the girls came to tell her they were expected in the Theatre in half an hour's time. "You'll be a great success, Venus," she said, "so don't be frightened."

"I am frightened of doing the wrong thing," Alicia replied, "and upsetting Mr. Bellow, who has been so kind to me."

"Oh, he thinks you're wonderful! I've never known him so touched over a newcomer as he is over you. In fact, we're all jealous."

Alicia smiled. "You need not be that. After all, I have a very limited performance, as I cannot remember all the things I ought to remember."

"It'll all come back to you," the girl said. "I remember hearing of a man who lost his memory for five years. Then suddenly it came back and he found he was a soldier and had been wounded in battle."

"I hope I do not have to wait five years," Alicia cried. "It is very kind of you all to help me and to be so understanding."

"If you ask me, it was the luckiest thing that ever happened, that you were on the train when poor Annie disappeared. It would have upset His Nibs a great deal more than it did if you hadn't been there to take her place."

"It must have been a shock to all of you," Alicia said. "What about Annie's parents, if she has any. Have they been told?"

"I suppose the Master'll tell them sooner or later," the girl replied. "But for the moment, all he wants to do is to please the Prince, and that's what you must do or it'll spoil his evening for him."

"I will do my best," Alicia assured her. She had thought the Prince very kind when he had come to the Theatre to meet them. He was certainly extremely good looking.

What she had not expected was that the song at the end of the show would be such a great success. The small audience had clapped and clapped until the Prince said: "It is no use, Bellow, we insist on having an encore."

No one was more delighted than Bellow, who

had quickly drawn back the curtains and told Venus to sing her song again. Yet this time, instead of playing the piano as she had done previously, the orchestra of three played the song very softly while she stood at the front of the stage and sang.

Because Venus looked so lovely, the Prince and his friends listened in complete silence. Each one of them was thinking she was aptly called Venus. They had never seen a more lovely Goddess.

The only evening dress which had been in her case was one she had brought with her to the Theatre because she thought she might have needed one before the rest of her clothes were unpacked. It was quite simple, yet extremely becoming to her. Made of a soft chiffon the color of her eyes, it was ornamented round the neck and at the back with very pale roses. Because it came from a famous dressmaker and was also the very latest fashion, it was a perfect frame for her beauty and her strangely gleaming fair hair. In fact, the Prince, watching her, thought he had never, in his life, seen anyone quite so beautiful.

It was extraordinary that she should be performing with traveling players who, though they had such a good reputation, were looked down upon by professional actors and actresses.

The curtain fell for the second time to great

applause. Then the Prince said to Bill Bellow, "Join us in my private Dining Room as soon as you can. Then I will tell you how much I appreciated your performance."

"Your Royal Highness is exceedingly kind," Bill Bellow replied. He bowed several times as the Prince led his party from the Theatre.

The girls were busy touching up their faces and rearranging their hair. But Alicia just stood by the piano wondering why she should remember that particular song. Also, why she should know it in French.

"Come along! Come along!" Bill Bellow said. "You mustn't keep His Royal Highness waiting. The others are ready."

"I am ready, too," Alicia murmured.

He hurried them along the passages which led to the Prince's private Dining Room. The Prince and his guests were already in the entre-salle, where there was champagne for the performers and fresh lemonade for those who did not drink, of which Venus was one.

As she sipped the lemonade, she was still trying to remember where she had heard the song which had pleased the Prince.

He came to her side, saying, "There is no need for me to tell you how beautifully you sing and what a lovely voice you have. You must have heard it a million times."

"If I did, I wish I could remember," Alicia said.

"I will always remember how you sang tonight," the Prince replied. "I want to hear you a great many more times before you leave."

She smiled at him. "You are very kind," she answered demurely, "and very encouraging."

"That is what I want to be," he answered.

A servant announced dinner and they walked into the next room. The Prince's private Dining Room was particularly well furnished. He had chosen a number of pictures from other parts of the Palace which he particularly liked. He was used to people praising them and telling him what good taste he had. But he had not expected a girl from the traveling players to recognize any of them.

He seated Venus on his right-hand side, saying, "Goddesses, of course, take precedence over everyone, and no one is more important than the Goddess of Love."

The men laughed at that. Then one of them said, "I've always admired Your Royal Highness's taste. At the same time, you're clever enough to have an explanation for it."

The others laughed at this. Alicia, however, was looking at the pictures. "I have always loved

Fragonard better than any other French painter,"
she said.

The Prince looked at her in surprise. "You have
been to France?" he asked.

"I remember that picture," she answered, "but I
do not remember being in France."

He thought it was a strange thing to say. He
would not have commented on it but Bill Bellow,
who was sitting only a seat away, bent forward and
said: "I forgot to tell Your Royal Highness that Venus was the one person in my flock who was
slightly hurt in the train crash. She is finding it
difficult to remember all the things she has done
before. But I told her it will all return in time."

"Of course it will," the Prince agreed. "I am
sorry you were hurt, although obviously not very
badly."

"It was on top of my head," Alicia said, "and I
do not remember things as I ought to."

"You are not to worry about anything tonight,"
the Prince commanded. "You have been absolutely
brilliant, and now we want to talk to you and make
you feel happy."

"As you make us feel happy," one of the men
who was listening piped in.

"I told you that I thought Mr. Bellow's show was
the best I have ever seen in my travels," the Prince

said. "It is a great delight for me to have you here tonight."

"It is a great delight for us to be here, Your Royal Highness," Bill Bellow replied.

The servants were already taking round the food. Alicia realized that the dishes were French. It made her say, "I am sure you have a French Chef, although I did not expect to find one here."

"That is very clever of you," the Prince said. "My Chef *is* French. I brought him back when I went to Paris. That, of course, was when I saw Mr. Bellow's show, but you were not with it."

"No, I suppose I was not," Alicia replied.

"You certainly make it even more marvelous than it was when I saw it in France," the Prince said, "and I was determined it should come to my country."

"And we're very pleased to be here," Mr. Bellow answered before Alicia could speak.

"Well, I am afraid you will have to give me many more performances than I expected," the Prince said. "There is no need for me to tell you we will enjoy every one of them."

Then everyone began to talk at once. There was no doubt that the Prince's guests were all delighted with the five girls who were seated among them. His Royal Highness, however, monopolized

Venus's attention. To his surprise they were talking
of pictures and books. He was aware that Venus
was very different from the other girls. They were
amusing and flirtatious with his friends. There was
no doubt that they were clever enough to keep the
men laughing. Yet he found himself with Venus
discussing things which she said to her own surprise she remembered but were entirely, he
thought later, intellectual.

He found it impossible to learn anything about
her, as he wished to do. "How long have you been
with Mr. Bellow?" he asked.

Alicia made a graceful but helpless gesture
with her hands. "I cannot . . . remember," she
answered.

"I can understand how annoying it must be,"
the Prince said sympathetically. "At the same time,
how could you remember that French song which
you sang so beautifully?"

There was silence for a moment. Then she said,
"I think I must have heard it in Paris. But all I can
really remember is the song itself."

Because he did not want to pressure her, he began to talk about his horses. He saw by the light in
her eyes how much it interested her. "Tomorrow I
will show you the Stables," he said. "As I have already told Mr. Bellow, if you want a horse or a

carriage to take you round the town it is at your disposal."

"When you talk like that I want to see every-thing," Alicia enthused. "I am sure, from what I have seen of it already, this is a very beautiful Palace."

"I like to think so," the Prince replied. "My Father and Mother spent a lot of time and money in bringing it up-to-date and making it far more comfortable and more beautiful than it had ever been in the past."

"Are all your pictures as exceptional as those in this room?" Alicia asked. "I am sure you will find me wandering all over the Palace where I have no right to be."

The Prince threw up his hands. "The Palace is at your disposal. Think of it as yours and tell me which of the many pictures, and there are a great number of them, you enjoy most."

"I would love to do that," Alicia said. "But I am sure we will have to rehearse and rehearse so as to be good enough performers when your Royal Highness wants to see us."

"There is no need for you to do that," the Prince said. "You are so beautiful that all I want to look at is you."

She gave a little laugh. "That is a very pretty speech. But having been told you are a Prince, I know there are great demands on you. You must be very busy."

"I expect to be far more busy than I am at the moment," the Prince said, thinking of his Wedding.

As he spoke, he wondered how much the players knew of what had been expected to happen when they were asked to Rasgrad. He had, in fact, made it clear to Bill Bellow that they were to entertain his guests when he was married. The fact that they had not asked him any questions made him think that they were aware, although they were too polite to say so, that the Bride was missing. They talked until dinner was finished. Then as the Ladies, in English fashion, left the Gentlemen to drink their port, Alicia found the piano, violin and drum had been moved into the Sitting Room.

There was an excellent floor from which the carpet had been removed, although the room was quite a small one. The chairs had all been placed on one side.

"So we are going to dance," Alicia said to one of the other girls.

"We usually do after a dinner like that," she

185

replied. "But the men we have tonight are a great deal better looking and much younger than we often find ourselves stuck with."

"That's true enough," another one chimed in. "I had an awful old prowler at the last place where we stayed. He was seventy if he was a day, and behaved as if he were a boy of twenty-one."

"But he gave you a very pretty bracelet," one of the others remarked. "So although he was unpleasant, it must have been worth it."

The girl who had first spoken shrugged her shoulders. "I have my feelings as well as they have theirs. I like a man to be tall, dark and handsome."

"Don't we all?" one of the others laughed. "But this lot goes to the top of the scoreboard and there's no mistake about that."

Listening, Alicia did not really know what they were talking about. Anyway, she was not particularly interested. She was still trying to remember where she had seen such beautiful pictures before and when. Somehow she still could not put a name to it. When she tried, she felt she was looking out into darkness.

They were shown into a bedroom where they could tidy themselves, and when they returned to the Prince's Sitting Room, the men were already there with Mr. Bellow standing by the piano. He ordered his very small orchestra to play the most up-to-date and modern dance tunes they knew. They started off with a dreamy waltz.

Almost before she was aware of it, Alicia was being taken round the room by the Prince. As they waltzed, she had the strange feeling it was something she had not only done before but wanted to do again.

"You dance divinely, as I expected," the Prince said. Then he drew her a little closer. But as he did so he felt a very strange feeling in his heart. It not only surprised him but made him aware that Venus was even more beautiful than he had thought her to be.

He had prided himself on knowing as soon as he looked into a woman's eyes or touched her hand whether she really meant anything to him or not. It was something he had questioned himself about finding it strange that another person's vibrations should be strong enough to affect his own. Yet undoubtedly, in his association with great Beauties all over the world, he had often found himself completely unresponsive to them—even if they were acknowledged as the loveliest women in Society.

Yet now, with this young woman, a performer in a traveling show, he felt as if every instinct in his body vibrated to her. They did not speak. They just moved round and round in the small room. Finally, as the music came to an end, the Prince drew Alicia out through the open window into the garden.

Tonight, almost as if it were a mocking recompense for its absence before, the moon was full, casting a silver light on the garden.

This part of the great garden behind the Palace was kept exclusively for the Prince. He often sat there when he was working and had no wish to be seen or interrupted by people in the other part of the garden. There was a large screen of flowering trees and bushes to keep it private, and the flowers themselves were the best and most beautiful his gardeners could provide.

In the center of the garden there was a small, exquisitely carved fountain that spouted water through the arms of a cupid. It was not only beautifully carved but was in fact, like the basin of the fountain, very old. Alicia gave a little gasp of delight and moved towards it.

"It is the most beautiful fountain I have ever seen," she said. "I know it is very old. In fact, it must have been here when the Palace was first built, which I know was over 200 years ago."

"Who told you that?" the Prince asked.

"One of the Equerries when I asked him the date of it," Alicia answered. "But I was sure before he told me that it was very old. You must be exceedingly proud of it."

"Of course I am," the Prince replied. "I am only surprised that you should know so much about pictures and old houses. What were you doing before you joined 'Bellow's Belles'?"

There was silence before Alicia said, "I am . . . trying to . . . remember but . . . it . . . just . . . evades . . . me."

"Then let us talk about ourselves," the Prince said. "As I have told you already, you are the most beautiful person I have ever seen. But you surprise me with everything you say."

"Why should I do that?" Alicia asked.

"Although I admire them very much, you are not like the other girls with whom you are performing."

"They have been very kind to me," Alicia said.

"How long have you known them?" the Prince asked.

Again there was silence.

"Never mind, let us talk about ourselves," the Prince suggested. "Tell me what you think about me."

Alicia looked up at him.

He thought in the moonlight that no one could look more lovely or more alluring.

"I do not think," she said softly, "you are really interested in what I think about you. Except, of course, a Prince has always got to be of great importance and I must be careful not to offend you."

"I think it would be impossible for you to do that," the Prince answered. "It is difficult to put into words, but I think when you were dancing with me just now I had never felt closer to anyone than I felt to you."

"You mean your vibrations touched mine," Alicia said.

It was what the Prince had been thinking himself. He stared at her in astonishment. "Did you feel what I felt?" he asked.

"What I felt," Alicia answered, "was something I have never felt before."

The Prince drew in his breath. He wanted to pull her close to him. He wanted to kiss her more than he had ever wanted to kiss any woman in his whole life. Yet it was impossible because they were not alone in the garden.

Then, as he looked down into Alicia's eyes, he was aware there was soft laughter not far away. One of the other girls came out through the open window into the garden. Just for a moment neither of them moved.

Then the Prince said, "We must talk about this when we are alone another time. Leave it to me; I will arrange it."

Alicia did not know exactly what he meant. She threw back her head to look at the water glistening in the moonlight as it was thrown up towards the sky from the fountain. She looked so lovely as she did so that the Prince could only draw in his breath. She was undoubtedly more exquisite and more exciting than anyone he could ever remember.

As he took her hand to draw her back into the lighted room where they were dancing, he wanted her more than he had ever wanted anyone before.

Although he hated to admit it, she had touched his heart.

7

Alicia woke up early because the sun was shining through the sides of the curtains. She looked at her clock and found it was not yet six o'clock, yet she had a sudden eagerness to be out in the sunshine.

She got up to get dressed and found, although she had not been aware of it, that her riding skirt had been in the case which had come with her to the Palace. She put it on, wearing only a thin muslin blouse above it. She hesitated as to whether she should take her hat but instead told herself in the early morning she was not likely to see anyone.

She ran down the stairs and finding everything quiet in the hall, let herself out into the garden.

For a moment she was enthralled with the flowers. Then she knew that more than anything else, she wanted to see the Prince's horses.

It was only a short walk through the garden to the Stables, which were on the far side of the Palace. As she expected because it was so early, there was only one sleepy young Groom keeping watch over the horses. He touched his forelock with his finger. Then he seemed uninterested in what she did.

She went from stall to stall, finding each horse more magnificent than the last. *How lucky he is,* she thought. *He can ride every day on these marvelous, well-bred horses.*

Then suddenly she remembered that he had said if any of them wanted to ride, the horses were at their disposal. She called the Groom and told him in his own language that she wanted to ride and asked him to get a sidesaddle.

He went to fetch one, leaving Alicia with the difficult task of choosing which horse she would ride. There were three which seemed more outstanding than the rest. Finally she chose one, and when the boy came back, he saddled the chosen horse for her and produced its bridle.

As she rode out of the Stables, she realized there was still no one about. The world outside the Palace was waiting for her.

She passed through a gate at which there were

two sentries who paid no attention to her, since she came from the Palace.

Then she was out into the open land. On one side there was a river and above it were the tall mountains which, until now, she had only seen in the distance. They were very picturesque; some of the peaks were still white with snow.

She galloped her horse until they were both breathless from the speed they went. Then she settled down to a quiet trot. She was fascinated by the butterflies which flew out of the grass in front of her, and by the birds she could hear overhead.

It seems enchanted, she thought. She wondered if she had ever seen anything like it before and, if so, where. Then she found herself, as she had before she went to sleep the night before, thinking of the Prince.

She could not explain to herself exactly what she felt when they had stood by the fountain in the garden. Yet it was so marvelous and so wonderful that she had thought about it until she had fallen asleep.

The feeling had still been there when she woke up in the middle of the night. *I am sure, if I had ever felt like that before,* she told herself, *I would remember it.*

It was difficult to put into words but she felt as if her whole being vibrated towards him, and she had the feeling that he felt the same towards her. She could again see his eyes in the moonlight. With the fountain playing behind him he looked, she thought, like Apollo.

She rode on to where, in the far distance, she could see trees. She hoped she'd find a forest. It was growing hot in the sunshine and she thought it would be wonderful to ride through a wood under the trees. Perhaps she would find, in the center of it, a pool like the one she had known . . .

She stopped suddenly. Where had she seen a pool in a wood before? Somehow she could see quite clearly the kingcups growing at the water's edge. Now she vaguely remembered seeing her own reflection where she had looked down seeking the water nymphs.

Where was it? Where was that place? She asked the questions again and again but found no answer. Then, as she drew nearer to the wood, although it was still some distance away, she looked back and saw, to her surprise, a man on a horse.

She did not know why, but as if she was prompted to wait for him, she turned her horse round. She saw him coming at a fast pace nearer and nearer. It was then she was aware it was the Prince. She felt a sudden throb in her breast, as if her heart had turned a somersault. As he reached her, he drew in his horse.

She smiled at him and he said, "I thought I would never find you. How could you have come so far so quickly?"

"I did not think anyone else would be riding so early in the morning," Alicia replied.

"I always ride early," the Prince said. "But last night, as I could not sleep, I am earlier than usual."

"Let us go into the wood," Alicia begged. "It looks so inviting, and I am wondering if there is a pool in it."

"There is and I will show it to you," the Prince answered.

He went ahead to show her the way into the wood. They were then riding their horses down a moss-covered path. The forest itself, Alicia thought, was exactly as she wanted it to be. There were small rabbits scurrying ahead of them, birds fluttered out of the trees and there was the scent of syringa. When they reached the pool it was exactly as she somehow remembered it. There were several water lilies floating on the water. The king-cups were yellow round the outside.

"Is that what you wanted?" the Prince asked in a deep voice.

"I have either dreamt of it or seen it before," Alicia answered. "But for the moment I cannot think where."

"I cannot believe that you want anything more attractive than this one," he said.

"No, of course not," she replied. "I am sure if the people in your town knew of it they would come here and throw in a coin and pray that their wish will come true."

The Prince put his hands into his pocket and drew out some money. "I want you to wish," he said, "and perhaps your wish will be the same as mine."

Alicia dismounted and knotted her reins. Then she walked to the edge of the pool. The Prince did the same.

Their horses, quite happy to look for grass, made no effort to leave, so the Prince and Alicia stood for a moment side by side, looking down into the water.

Then the Prince said in a deep voice, "What are you wishing for?"

"I suppose I am wishing for happiness like any-one else would," Alicia replied after a moment's pause.

"That is what I want," the Prince said, "but for me it can never come true."

"Why not?" Alicia asked. As she looked up at the Prince, the words seemed to focus on her lips.

"I love you," the Prince declared. "I love you as I have never loved anyone before, and I know that you are who I have been looking for all my life."

Alicia's eyes widened but she did not reply.

Then he went on, "I have traveled a great deal and I have seen women I thought were beautiful who attracted me. But I have never seen anyone as lovely and as perfect as you."

Alicia was listening to him as if she were hypno-tized. Her eyes were held by his; it was impossible to look away.

"I love you, I love you," the Prince said. "I knew it from the first moment I saw you, but I realized last night you were as out of reach as if you were the Goddess Venus."

"Why?" Alicia asked. The words merely touched her lips, hardly making a sound.

"Because I am not a free man," the Prince re-plied. Now his voice was harsh, and there was a pain in it which she could feel.

"I have looked for you and dreamt of you," he went on. "Now you are here and it is difficult to believe you are real. But I have to send you away."

"I do . . . not . . . understand," Alicia murmured.

"Why should you?" he asked. "It is because I am not a free man. Because of the way I was born, my country must come first, and my true feelings are insignificant beside one word, which is *Duty*."

Because the pain in his voice hurt him in some strange way she could not understand, she turned her head to look at the pool. For a moment there was complete silence between them. Neither of them moved.

Then the Prince said, as if he were speaking his thoughts aloud, "I will tell Bill Bellow you must leave tonight or first thing in the morning, but preferably tonight. Then when we go back to the Palace, I will not see you again."

"But I . . . want to . . . see . . . you," Alicia said. "Why must . . . you . . . send me . . . away?"

"I thought you understood," the Prince told her. "I thought people would have told you that I am to marry immediately, only she has not arrived, an English girl who has been sent to me by Queen Victoria."

Alicia put her hand up to her forehead. "I have
. . . heard of that . . . before," she said, almost
as if she were speaking to herself.

"That is not surprising," the Prince answered.
"Many Balkan States have been saved from the
Russians by receiving the protection of England,
and that is what I and my Prime Minister have
asked for."

"So . . . you are . . . going to . . . be . . .
married?" Alicia murmured. It was as if she still
found it hard to understand what he was saying.

"I am going to be married as soon as my Bride
arrives," the Prince replied. "It might be today,
tomorrow or longer. But because sooner or later
she will arrive, I must send you away."

"But why? Why must I go?" Alicia asked.

"Because I love you and I want you more than I
have ever wanted anything in my whole life," the
Prince answered. "You are perfect and what I have
seen only in my dreams and thought I would
never find if I live to be a hundred."

He spoke with a depth in his voice which she
had not heard before. Instinctively she put out her
hand towards him. To her surprise he stepped
back.

"You must not touch me," he said. "I knew last

night, when we danced together, that I wanted you close to me. When we were in the moonlight I wanted to kiss you and tell you of my love."

"I thought that when I was singing to you," Alicia murmured.

"Oh, my Darling, my Sweet!" the Prince said. "How can you be so perfect and so wonderful in every way? I cannot imagine anything more like Heaven than teaching you about love."

Because of the way he spoke and the depth in his voice, Alicia turned her head to look again at the water.

"Because I am a man," the Prince said, "I want to kiss you and make you mine and defy the whole world to take you from me."

He gave a deep sigh before he went on, "But I am also a reigning Prince, and I cannot allow my country to be usurped and conquered by the Russians."

He drew in his breath and continued, "I want you, but because you are perfection itself, I cannot offer you anything that will spoil the wonder of you. As I cannot offer you anything but my heart, I have to send you away."

"But I want to stay," Alicia whispered.

"My Precious, you do not understand," the

Prince said. "If you stay you would lose, not only your innocence, but the dignity that is instinctively yours."

After a moment he went on as if he were talking to himself. "If you were an ordinary girl working for Bill Bellow as those others are, I could, I suppose, secretly make love to you."

Alicia turned her head to look at him as if she had not thought of this before.

Then he went on, "It would not only spoil you, but it would be an appalling way for me to welcome the woman who has been sent to save my country. So, my Darling, my Precious, you have to go away!"

"Now I understand," Alicia said. "But I know I will never feel for any man what I am feeling now."

For a moment the Prince could only look at her. It was with almost superhuman strength that he resisted taking her into his arms.

"I want to think of you," he said, "as I see you now. As a part of the wood with the flowers and the water. I suppose one day you will find a man whom you will love and marry. Then you will forget me."

"I do not think I will ever do that," Alicia whispered. "I know what . . . I am . . . feeling

now . . . is . . . different in every . . . way
. . . from anything . . . I . . . have . . . ever
known. It is . . . love . . . the real love . . .
which comes . . . from the . . . Gods themselves
. . . and I . . . do not . . . want to . . . lose
. . . it."

"And I do not want to lose you," the Prince said.
"But I have been told, ever since I was born, that
my Duty to my country is more important than
anything else, including my own feelings. Therefore, we have to say goodbye!"

For a moment neither of them spoke. Then he
said, "Perhaps one day, if God is merciful, we
might find each other again. But, for the moment,
I could not spoil anything as perfect as you."

He gave a deep sigh before he said, "Nor could
I behave in a manner which the English would not
consider correct from a Gentleman towards the
woman who is to be his wife."

"But . . . you . . . will think . . . of me . . .
and . . . I . . . will pray that . . . you . . . will
be . . . happy," Alicia whispered.

"I do not think that is likely," the Prince said.
"But let us both wish that God will be kind to us in
the future, and then we must go back."

He drew out again from his pocket the money
he had put back when they had dismounted. He

held it out to Alicia. She took a gold coin, kissed it, then held it against her lips. Then, shutting her eyes, she prayed with a fervency she had never known before that one day she and the Prince would be together again. As she threw the coin into the pool, the still water rippled away from it.

The Prince, who had been watching her, did the same. He took the largest and most valuable coin into his hand, touched it with his lips, then threw it into the water. For a moment they were still.

Alicia was praying with all her heart and soul that in the future she would meet the Prince again. "Every night . . . that we . . . are . . . apart," she said aloud, "before I . . . go . . . to . . . sleep I shall . . . wish upon . . . a . . . star . . . that God . . . will . . . bring . . . us . . . together."

"And I will do the same," the Prince assured her.

I love him, she thought as she turned to walk back to where her horse was waiting.

As Alicia stood patting him, the Prince picked her up in his arms and lifted her into the side-saddle.

She looked down at him and he said, "I love you! I love you with my body, my heart and my soul. You fill my whole world. There will never be anyone else but you."

He did not wait for her to reply. He merely walked away and, mounting his horse, rode off. There was nothing she could do but follow him.

As they left the wood, they galloped some way in silence. Then, as if the horses knew they should calm down and go a little slower, they gradually ended up walking with the river just below them. It was then that Alicia turned to look at the Prince. She saw the pain in his eyes and the expression on his face which told her more forcibly than words what he was feeling. She would have put out her hand, but she knew he did not want to touch her.

"We have to believe that our prayers will be answered," Alicia said very softly.

"We may have to wait," he said savagely, "what to me will be a hundred thousand years."

"I am . . . sure . . . because . . . we were . . . together . . . in that . . . lovely wood . . . and you . . . told . . . me you . . . loved me . . . that . . . somehow things . . . will come . . . right." She threw back her head as she had done the previous night and looked up at the sky.

"I know God is listening to us," she murmured. She was so lovely and the way she spoke was so moving that the Prince could only look at her. There were no words to express what he was feeling.

"If . . . I have . . . to go . . . away," Alicia said, after what seemed a very long time, "I . . . will . . . think of . . . you here . . . by your . . . river . . . with your . . . mountains above . . . you . . . and know that . . . you are . . . a very . . . good and . . . upright . . . person."

"I only wish I was different," the Prince replied.

Alicia shook her head. "No, you do not! You know what you are doing is right and I think, because right always wins in the end, our wishes will come true and the stars will bring us together."

"I love you!" the Prince said quietly. "I love everything you say, everything you do, how you look."

She smiled at him and he said, "I want to remember you like that. I think it is engraved on my heart." Then, as if he could bear it no longer, he spurred his horse.

He set off at a quick pace that was difficult for Alicia to keep up with. It was only when the Palace came in sight that the Prince slowed down.

"Goodbye, my Darling!" he said. "If you leave tonight, as I intend, think of me before you go to sleep, when I will be thinking of you."

Alicia did not reply immediately. Then she said very softly in French, " *Je t'adore! Je t'adore!* "

The sentries came to attention and the Prince passed by them first, with Alicia following him. Then, as they reached the gate into the Stables, he looked at her once again and said, "Leave that song with me. I will have it played to me every night."

"Then I will sing it every night," Alicia said softly. "Somehow I think . . . even though . . . we are . . . far apart, you . . . will . . . hear . . . me."

She did not wait for the Prince to answer but rode ahead. There were several Grooms waiting for them.

As the young man who had saddled her horse took him from her, Alicia walked out of the Stables. She was thinking of the Prince and had somehow forgotten her way. She soon found herself near the fountain where they had been last night. Almost instinctively both of them walked towards it.

As they stood with the water shooting up into the sky above them, the Prince said, "This was where I knew last night I loved you and because of that love, you would have to leave."

"I knew . . . but I . . . really did . . . not

. . . understand . . . that I . . . loved you," Alicia whispered.

"How could Fate be so cruel to us?" the Prince asked. "If I had never seen you, you would have remained in my dreams and not tortured me as you are torturing me now."

"I had no idea," Alicia said in a very small voice, "that love was so marvelous. Now when I am near you and when you are talking to me, I feel somehow that I have almost reached the stars."

"That is what I feel, too," the Prince replied. "But the world stands between us and because we cannot be together, we must both suffer, as far as I am concerned, unbearably."

Alicia looked up at the water glistening in the sun and said, "You may think I am very silly, but somehow I know our dreams will come true and our love, because it is so very, very wonderful, will never be wasted."

It was impossible for the Prince to find words in which to express what he was feeling. He, therefore, turned towards the Palace. As he stiffened, she knew he was walking back to his Duty, his country. She walked beside him. A footman inside the Palace saw them coming and opened the door. It was the main entrance leading inside from the garden. Opposite, at the very end of the great Hall, was the main entrance to the Palace.

As they walked in, side by side, they saw someone being received by the Lord Chamberlain and several Equerries. He was a tall man who was walking slowly from a carriage outside into the Palace. He had a stick in his hand. Then the Prince heard the Lord Chamberlain say to the visitor, "It is a great surprise to see Your Grace. But we are, of course, delighted that you are well enough to make the journey!"

As he spoke, the Prince realized who had arrived and in a low voice said to Alicia, "It is the Duke of Templeton. I had no idea he was well enough to travel."

As he moved forward to greet the Duke, to his astonishment, Alicia gave a cry which seemed to echo round the hall as she rushed forward. "Papa! Papa!" she cried. "You have come! I remember you!" The Duke put his arm round his daughter and kissed her.

"I was afraid you might be married without me," he said. "So I insisted that I was well enough to travel. The Doctors allowed me to do so, as long as I brought a Nurse with me, who has been most attentive. In fact, I am almost myself again."

"Oh, Papa, it is wonderful to see you. I lost my memory and could not remember who I was. But now that I have seen you it has all come back."

She realized as she finished speaking that everyone round them was silent and staring at them in astonishment. Then the Prince said in a strange voice, "Can it really be true, Your Grace, that this is your daughter?"

"Of course she is my daughter," the Duke answered, "and I have been worried in case I was too late to give her away when you were married. But they have told me the Ceremony has not yet taken place."

"It will take place now," the Prince said. "In fact, it will be tomorrow."

Those listening stared at him. Alicia, with tears in her eyes, said in a whisper that only he could hear, "I . . . told . . . you the . . . stars would . . . make . . . our . . . wishes . . . come true."

Because everything had been planned for the Wedding before the rail crash, it was not difficult to set the wheels in motion for the Ceremony to take place the following day.

Heralds went through the town telling the people that the Prince was being married to a relation of Queen Victoria of Great Britain. The Lord

Chamberlain was giving orders in the Palace from breakfast until it was time for dinner. The only person who was sad at the news and, in fact, who suffered from it was Bill Bellow.

"How could I have suspected," the Prince asked him, when they were alone, "that you had my future wife among your performers?"

Bill Bellow explained how Annie had been killed, although they had not been aware of it until several days after the accident. They were at the Palace before they realized that Alicia was not Annie.

"I am sure you thought," the Prince said, "that the exchange was very much to your advantage."

Bill Bellow laughed. "Of course I did," he said. "As Your Royal Highness is aware, she's the most beautiful creature I have ever seen."

"I agree with you," the Prince murmured.

"I knew that everyone who was in our audience would think the same," Bill Bellow went on. "In fact, I am just wondering how I can possibly find someone to fill her place."

"I will be very annoyed," the Prince said, "if there is not a girl in my country pretty enough to please you."

He smiled as he went on, "I must, of course, thank you for your kindness to Lady Frederika.

Having lost her memory, she might have got into bad hands and not been treated as kindly and with the understanding that 'Bellow's Belles' gave her."

He then gave Bill Bellow a check which made him gasp with surprise and excitement. He told him that he expected him to perform at the Palace Theatre, also at the Theatre located in the town every other night.

"I want the people of Rasgrad to see you and, of course, your lovely 'Belles.' "

"I am very grateful to Your Royal Highness," Bill Bellow said. "At the same time, it'll be impossible to replace Her Ladyship."

"She is unique," the Prince agreed.

When the Prince learned that her Father always called her Alicia, he had said, "As that is your name I like the best and which I would wish my people to call you, it will come first in the Marriage Service."

Alicia agreed to this, as she had always thought her other two names were dull and rather heavy. The Duke had been delighted because he said Alicia was not only his beloved child but her name was one he had always connected with her, and he would be sad to lose it.

Alicia put on her dress for dinner. She thought nothing could be more wonderful than that her

Father had arrived and she was to be married to-morrow to the man she really loved, who she now knew loved her.

She had always been afraid that one day she would marry someone who did not really love her. It would have been known as a broken marriage. To her, it would have broken her heart.

I love him, I love him, she thought happily as she dressed herself.

The maid helped her into one of the beautiful gowns which was to be part of her trousseau. She then had a quick glance to see if her Wedding Dress was all right. She hoped it had not been damaged in the train crash.

I want to look lovely on my Wedding Day, she thought to herself. *In fact, more beautiful than I have ever looked so that however old I become, he will always remember me as he saw me then.*

They had dinner on their own, as the Prince knew it would be a great mistake to have anyone except himself, the Bride and the Bride's Father there.

It was a meal at which they all laughed a lot. Alicia could not help thinking that no woman could have two more handsome men to talk to, and to laugh with.

They were just finishing dinner, which they had

eaten fairly early because the Prince thought it would be a mistake for Alicia's Father to stay up late after the long journey. It was important that he should be in good health tomorrow, as he was an essential part of the Wedding.

They were leaving the Dining Room when an Officer came hurrying up to the Prince. "I think I ought to tell Your Royal Highness," he began, "that the Russians are pouring into the City."

He paused for a moment before he went on, "They heard that His Grace arrived alone, and they think that as his daughter was not accompanying him, the marriage will now not take place. They are, therefore, determined to take possession of the country immediately."

The Prince was silent for a moment. Then he said, "Arrange for an open carriage. I will come down and see the people for myself."

"And I will come with you," Alicia said.

The Prince looked at her in surprise. "Do you mean that?" he asked.

"Of course I mean it!" she exclaimed. "They think I do not exist, so they have to see me. I will be quite safe if I am with you."

She slipped her hand into his as she spoke. They looked into each other's eyes, and for a moment it was difficult to remember what else was

happening. Then Alicia said, "What I must have—
and I am sure you have one handy—is a really
impressive diadem."

"Of course we have one," the Prince replied.
"My Mother's jewelry is always kept in the safe in
my private Sitting Room."

The Officer, who had been listening, hurried
off.

Then the Prince asked, "Are you really brave
enough to come with me?"

He lowered his voice as he said, "It may be unpleasant if the Russians are trying to take over.
There are a number of people in the City whom
they have already aroused who are also prepared
to make trouble."

"I will not be afraid if I am with you," Alicia
replied. As he smiled at her, she felt as if the sun
were shining outside instead of the moon.

The Officer came hurrying back with a very impressive diadem in his hand. It was a circlet covered with large diamonds which went over the top
of the head. When the Prince put it on her head,
Alicia knew that she looked not only like a Fairy
Queen but Royal, which was what she wanted at
the moment. The Officer, very sensibly, had also
brought with him a magnificent diamond necklace
with five rows of diamonds. When the Prince put it

round Alicia's neck, it made her sparkle as if she were a star which had fallen from the sky.

Then there was the cloak of blue velvet which was her own and matched the color of her eyes. Once Alicia and the Prince got into the carriage, she pushed it back so that everyone could see the necklace as well as the diadem on her head.

When she kissed her Father goodbye, he said, "Take care of yourself, Dearest. I have not come all this way to lose you."

"I am sure we will come back to you, Papa. Go to bed so that you are at your best tomorrow when we get married."

She looked up at him and added, "I want it to be a very wonderful Ceremony, one which I will always remember."

The carriage, drawn by four white horses, moved slowly away from the door. Behind them was a Regimental Band. It was followed by a Company of soldiers. There were a few people in the streets leading up to the Palace. The horses went quite quickly. In fact, Alicia looked back to see if the Band and the soldiers were still there.

When they got nearer to the City, they could hear the crowd long before they reached it.

She knew that the people had gathered in the great Square at the end of which was the

Cathedral, where she was to be married tomorrow. It was then, as the carriage moved slowly forward until it reach the center of the Square, that people who were nearest to them stared in astonishment at Alicia. She knew they had been told by the Russians that she was not there and the Wedding would not take place.

As the carriage came to a standstill in the center of the Square, there were shouts and screams from the other end of it. Alicia realized the Russians were pouring in through the gates of the City. She was certain, although it was too far for her to see, that it had been forced open and they were flooding in. They were making the people of Rasgrad realize that they were the conquerors and had to be obeyed. Still, when the people round the carriage were aware the Prince and his future Bride were there, they made a feeble attempt at cheering them.

The Prince stood looking backwards so that he could see at least half of the Square. He began to speak in a very strong voice, which rang out as he said, "My people, I am here tonight to bring you someone who has just arrived from England with the blessing of Her Majesty Queen Victoria. Tomorrow, we will be married at the Cathedral. I ask you all to come and wish us happiness. As you well

217

know, under the protection of Her Majesty, we will be safe and also encouraged to make ourselves one of the most important, and richest, countries in the Balkans."

There were cheers at this, but there was still a great deal of noise at the other end of the Square. Alicia was afraid the encroaching Russians might suddenly try to seize the Prince and perhaps take him prisoner. She moved a little nearer to him.

He put his arm round her as he said, "Here I have Her Majesty Queen Victoria's gift to Rasgrad in the shape of the most lovely and the most beautiful Princess you have ever seen. She wants to meet you all and to love you. I know together we will make this one of the happiest countries there has ever been. Let me, therefore, introduce you to my future wife, who will rule this country with me. Her name is Princess Frederika. She is in fact the Queen's Goddaughter."

Alicia smiled and waved her hand. The people nearest to the carriage cheered.

Then the Prince said, "Now I want to speak to the men who served my Father and who I hope will serve me and my son, who I trust will follow after me."

There were cheers at this. Alicia thought the noise at the other end of the Square was not quite

so loud. She thought perhaps the people were eager to hear the Prince. They were, therefore, not
as interested in the Russians as they had been
when they first arrived.

"We have done so much in the past to make
Rasgrad great, and I think now with your help and
the help of my beautiful Bride it will be even
greater. There is nothing we cannot do if we set
our hearts to it."

While he was talking and Alicia was standing
close to him and still holding his hand, she saw a
man a little way back in the crowd. He was climbing onto the base of one of the statues which ornamented the Square. In the nearby lamplight, she
saw him slip and thought for a moment he would
fall. Then she realized he was hampered by having
something in his hand.

The Prince was still speaking, but she was so
concentrating on what the man was doing on the
statue that she missed some of the things the
Prince was saying. It was then, as the man stood up
and steadied himself against the statue of someone
who had been great in the past, that she realized
he had a gun in his hand.

It suddenly went through her mind that if he
aimed at the Prince, who was now standing in the
open carriage, it would be almost impossible for

him to miss. Frantically, she looked round and saw behind them, on the seat on which they had been sitting, that the Prince had brought with him a small pistol. It was not unlike the one her Father owned, which he had shown her how to fire.

There were now tremendous cheers at something the Prince had said. As the people waved their hands, she bent down and picked up the pistol. As she steadied herself and the Prince continued with what he was saying, the man on the statue brought his gun up to his shoulder and aimed at the Prince. Swiftly, because she always moved so quickly, Alicia lifted the pistol up in the way her Father had shown her. She fired at the Russian who was about to kill the Prince. Because she had become, at her Father's insistence, an excellent shot, she hit him in the forehead just above his eyes.

As he fell backwards, his gun went off. At the explosion, everyone turned their heads to see what had happened. Only as he fell did they realize the man was a Russian and that the shot from the carriage had prevented him from killing their Prince. There was a roar of indignation.

The Prince, who had not had the slightest idea what was happening beside him, put his arms round Alicia and drew her close to him. "You saved my life, my Darling," he said. "Only you could be so clever."

It was then as he held her close and his lips were on hers that the people went crazy. They shouted and screamed with delight. It was then the Russian was pulled from the statue, and a dozen men trod on him deliberately.

The Prince was to learn later that the soldiers had driven the Russians, who were pouring in through the North entrance, back the way they had come.

When the Russians were finally all out of the City or else dead on the ground, the soldiers locked the gates and bolted them so that no one else could enter until morning. The Prince and Alicia were not aware of this at the moment. They could only respond to the cheering and excitement of the crowd by waving their hands and thanking those nearest to them.

Some of the people insisted on shaking hands, so both the Prince and Alicia leaned over the side of the carriage. It was then the Band, which had been silent, broke into the National Anthem, and everyone stood to attention and sang with the earnestness and joy which came from their very hearts. It was as the Anthem finished that the Prince gave the order for the carriage to drive round the Square before taking them home.

The Band broke into one of the tunes which were popular at the time, prompting some of the people to dance as they waved to the Prince and Alicia. Others ran after the carriage so that they could touch their hands before the horses carried them farther on. It was a most triumphant and exciting occasion.

Only when they left the City behind them and were driving quietly towards the Palace did the Prince say, "How could you have been so wonderful, my Darling? Everyone knows now that I am marrying someone who will not only make *me* happy but them as well. You are wonderful, really wonderful!"

"It was so lucky I saw him," Alicia replied. "I was terrified he might kill you."

"So you killed him," the Prince said. "Who taught you to be such a marvelous shot?"

"Who do you think?" she asked. "My Father, of course. He is a first-class shot just as he is a marvelous rider. I am longing for him to see your horses."

"First of all we have to have our Honeymoon,"

the Prince retorted. "And that, I can promise you, is very important to me."

"Where are you taking me?" Alicia asked.

"That is a secret," he replied, "and I will not tell you until we are married in the Cathedral and I know then you are really mine and cannot disappear or fly away into the sky."

He looked up at the stars and gave a deep sigh. "How could I have known when I was saying goodbye to you that this could happen? I do not know how to express my gratitude to those who have heard the wish I made upon the star."

"My wish has been answered, too," Alicia replied. For a moment, she laid her cheek against his shoulder as she said, "I wanted you because I already loved you. I had no idea it was possible since I thought I was just a performer in Bill Bellow's show."

"It is something, my Darling, you will never do again," the Prince replied. "But we will make certain that they come to us at least once a year and entertain our people and perhaps inspire in them the same happiness that you brought to me the moment I first saw you."

Alicia drew in her breath. "Did you really fall in love with me the moment you saw me?" she asked.

"At first glance I did not think you were real," the Prince answered. "Then, when I came on the stage and looked into your eyes, I knew you were the most beautiful woman I had ever seen. You mattered to me more than I could express in words or even in thoughts."

"Oh, Darling, I am so happy," Alicia murmured. "I want more than I have ever wanted anything in the world to be your wife."

"That is what you will be tomorrow," the Prince replied. He kissed her hand as he finished speaking.

She felt a throb in her heart which told her without words how much she loved him.

8

The Church Bells of Rasgrad were ringing out the next morning. The Band was playing, and in some miraculous way the people of the town managed to decorate their houses and their trees. They dressed themselves up, as well, to celebrate the marriage of their Royal Ruler to the most beautiful Bride they had ever seen.

When the gold coach, drawn by four white horses, went slowly through the streets, there were exclamations of astonishment at Alicia's beauty. Both the men and the women realized that the new Princess would be the envy of every country around them.

"It is so wonderful of you to come, Papa," Alicia said as they drove to the Church. She did not say any more. But she thought that one day she would tell him how she and the Prince had fallen in love with each other. How, because he loved her too much to cheapen her, he was going to send her away.

Only a man who understood real love could have done that, she said to herself.

There were children standing on the steps which led up to the Cathedral. As Alicia and the Duke moved up the stairs—slowly, because he was using his stick—the children threw rose petals in front of them. And when they went through the West Door of the Cathedral even more children rushed forward to scatter yet more rose petals at their feet.

Father and daughter were moving slowly up the aisle when Alicia saw the Prince waiting at the top near the Altar. She felt as if every vibration in her body went out to his and she knew he felt the same.

When he finally put the ring on her finger, he felt a quiver go through her. He knew that their love was increasing minute by minute, hour by hour. There was, however, a great deal to do before they could be together. The Marriage Service, on the Prince's instructions, was not too long, but very moving.

After it ended, Alicia walked slowly back down the aisle, on the Prince's arm, feeling very proud, and very moved. When they reached the top of the steps which led down to where their carriage was waiting, cheers came from everyone in the Square. There were no noisy Russians as there had been last night to make the Prince fear that his country was being taken over.

Alicia, although she tried not to, could not help looking at the statue where she had killed the Russian who attempted to kill her Prince. To her delight, instead of the statue, all she could see were flowers. The people of the City had been up very early to decorate the Square with a mass of flowers.

Now instead of seeing, as she had feared, the place where she had killed the man, she only saw white, pink, blue and yellow flowers, which shone like stars in the sunshine.

They drove back to the Palace in the open carriage. By the time their journey came to an end, the carriage, too, was almost filled with flowers.

There was, of course, a large party of distinguished visitors and Members of the Cabinet waiting for them. They drank to the couple's health, and the Prince made an excellent speech, announcing that this was the happiest and most wonderful day of his life.

Because Alicia knew he sincerely meant it and it was not just something any Bridegroom might say, as he sat down she lifted her face to his.

As they looked at each other, everyone in the room felt lumps come suddenly to their throats because the scene was so touching: It was obvious the two young people were ecstatically happy.

Alicia changed into her "going away" dress, even though she still had no idea where they were going or what she should wear. She had merely told the maids to pack a number of her prettiest and most attractive gowns in one of the cases. She could only hope that she would not be wrongly dressed for whatever happened on their Honeymoon.

When Alicia went downstairs, her Father was waiting to wish her goodbye. Most of the Courtiers as well as the Prime Minister and Members of the Cabinet were there, too, and Alicia shook hands with all of them.

Everyone told her that she was the most beautiful Princess they had ever imagined and that Rasgrad was very lucky to have her.

Finally, with a last kiss to her Father, she got into the carriage, which was waiting outside. They drove off amid cheers and cries of "Good luck" and "God bless you" from their guests.

Only as they went through the Palace gates did Alicia slip her hand into the Prince's and say, "I have no idea where we are going on our Honey-moon."

"It is a surprise, a special surprise," he replied, "which I will be very sorry if you do not enjoy."

As she knew he wanted to keep it a secret, she did not press him any further. She merely told him, not only in words but with the expression in her eyes, how much she loved him.

To her surprise, they traveled some distance from the City before stopping at a wide river which she had not known existed. As the carriage drew closer she saw there was a small but very modern and attractive yacht ahead of them.

She looked at the Prince and he smiled. He knew what she was asking him. "We are going to the sea," he said. "This is the one river we can travel on which takes us out of the Balkans and onto the Sea of Marmara."

"I had no idea there was such a thing!" Allela exclaimed. "And, of course, I am thrilled to be on a yacht with you."

"We will be completely on our own with no crowds to stare at us," the Prince said. "As you know, my Darling, I want you entirely to myself."

He paused before he added, "I also want not only your beautiful body but your thoughts, your prayers and everything else which makes up my wife."

He said the last word as if it were a caress. She would have kissed him if she had not been aware that the carriage had come to a standstill and the Captain of the yacht and most of the Crew were waiting for them to board.

The yacht was more attractive than any yacht Alicia had ever seen. It had been designed by the Prince himself for those times when he felt he must get away from all the difficulties and troubles of his country and have a quiet holiday.

"As you can imagine," he told her, "I have visited Constantinople and a great number of other places in the Mediterranean which I know will thrill you."

"I am thrilled with it all," Alicia answered excitedly. "It is the most lovely toy any spoiled young boy could possibly ask for."

They were alone in the cabin when the Prince said, "If you are going to be unkind to me I will kiss you until you tell me once again you love me."

"I do not have to kiss you to tell you that," Alicia replied. "I love you, I love you. Oh, Darling, could anything be more marvelous than this?"

She paused for a moment. Then she went on,

"It is what I dream of and what I hoped might happen, yet it seemed that everything was against me."

The Prince knew she was thinking of the moment when she was told she had to marry a man she had never seen merely because he had applied to Queen Victoria for help.

He kissed her until she whispered, "I love you, I love you. I think, Darling, I must explore your beautiful yacht. Otherwise I will not meet those who are going to make our Honeymoon the happiest one that has ever taken place."

They had luncheon, which was delicious. When Alicia saw the Wedding Cake, she was not surprised to learn that the Chef the Prince had arranged to have on his yacht was a Frenchman.

"Everything I have eaten is so delicious," Alicia said, "that I can only wonder what he will think of for dinner."

"By the time we have dinner," the Prince replied, "we will be at the end of the river and in the sea. I only hope it is not rough."

"You need not worry about me," Alicia said. "I have been to sea with Papa and I was not sick once even though we did go through the Bay of Biscay."

"How can you always be different from every

other woman I have ever known?" the Prince asked. "Everything about you is so lovable and so exquisite, I still think I am dreaming."

They had been kissing each other for most of the afternoon. The Prince had still not made her his as she had expected he would. She had a feeling he had a reason for not doing so and, therefore, did not ask questions.

It was only after she had changed for dinner and the sun was sinking in the sky that she went to the Saloon to find that there was a delicious dinner waiting for them. Every course seemed somehow to express the joy and delight of their Wedding Day.

"It is all so wonderful," Alicia whispered. Then the last course was finished and they were alone.

"There is one thing I want to show you before we go to bed," the Prince said.

"Another surprise?" she asked.

"I think it is one you will enjoy perhaps more than anything else," he answered.

She realized the yacht had come to a standstill. Then she heard the anchor going down. "Where have we stopped?" she asked.

"Come and look for yourself," the Prince replied.

They went out on deck. There was a full moon

climbing up the sky and the stars were just begin-
ning to appear. Then she saw they were in a small
harbor where the land was not very high above
them.

"I want you to come ashore," the Prince said.

She was rather surprised but was only too willing to do anything he wanted. Taking her by the
hand, he drew her down. She found that they
were in a little bay with a very small beach. The
sailors had already made a way for them to walk
from the side of the yacht onto the ground.

It seemed a little precarious, so the Prince went
first and held her hand. She managed to reach the
ground quite easily.

There were a lot of trees coming into blossom.
Nevertheless, even as she reached the ground, she
felt something strange, which she had never felt
before. They walked on under the trees until she
saw that the Island on which they had landed was
larger than she had at first thought, and at the far
end of it was something she could not recognize in
the dim light. But she felt it was of some importance.

"Where are we?" she asked.

"Could I bring you anywhere," the Prince
answered, "but to the Island of the King of
Love."

"You mean this is Apollo's Island?" she asked incredulously.

"Of course it is," the Prince replied. "I knew you would want to come here. I have been here so often hoping and praying that one day I would find you." It was then he put his arms round her and kissed her.

Alicia remembered reading what Apollo's Mother had felt when he was born. She was sure that, because the Prince was kissing her, she was feeling the same thing. Alicia knew that to celebrate Apollo's birth, the islands exploded in holy joy, strange perfumes filled the air and white swans suddenly appeared on the water.

She was aware there were strange lights glittering and shining high up in the air towards the stars.

After they returned to the yacht, she undressed and got into bed. When everything was very quiet, except for the soft lapping of the sea against the side of the yacht, the Prince came into her cabin. He was wearing a long, dark, almost military-style robe. There was only the light of the moon coming through the portholes.

For a moment he stood looking at her and said,

"I am sure this is a dream and I am terrified that I might wake up."

"It is a dream we have both dreamt, Darling," Alicia said. "I told you if we wished upon a star our wishes would come true. God has been very kind to us."

The Prince blew out the candles, then got into bed and took Alicia in his arms. He could just barely see her in the moonlight, but he knew that every time he looked at her she was more lovely than she had been a minute before. Then very gently, because it was a mistake to be in a hurry when dealing with perfection, he allowed his lips to find hers. At the mere touch of them, she felt her whole body come alive with their love, and he felt the same.

As his kisses became more demanding, she knew that this was what she had longed for. It would be impossible for her ever to feel the same for any other man.

"I . . . love . . . you," she said very softly. Then, almost as if he had asked her to do so, she said in French, " 'Je t'adore!' "

"And I love you, my Beautiful One," the Prince said. "There will never be enough words in either of our languages to tell you how much."

His voice deepened as he went on, "But I think

235

we both know that we are the other half of each other. This is something I have been looking for all my life, and now I have found it in you."

"I know . . . you are . . . the other . . . half of me," Alicia said. "And . . . a very . . . marvelous half."

"Can anything be more perfect?" the Prince asked. "When we have our children they will be perfect, too, because we will have made them and we have been blessed by God in finding each other and becoming husband and wife."

Then he was kissing her again. Kissing her wildly, passionately and demandingly. She knew he had been afraid he would lose her.

"I love you! I love you!" he said a thousand times.

Then, he gently made her his, carrying her up to the stars. The Angels were singing because they knew how happy the two young lovers were. Somehow, because their feelings for each other were so strong, their emotions lifted them out of the world into the Heaven of the Gods, where they did not need to speak.

As his lips came down on hers, she felt every nerve in her body respond to him. They were not two people but one, united by the glory and wonder of the God of Love himself. As the Prince and

Alicia gave themselves to each other, they knew
they had touched the stars. Everything they had
longed for, all they had prayed for had come true.

"I love you, I love you," Alicia wanted to say.
But there was no need for words.

Together, they had found the real love which all
people seek. The love which comes from God, and
is part of God. Because they had been Blessed, it
was theirs for Eternity.

ABOUT THE AUTHOR

BARBARA CARTLAND, the world's best known and bestselling author of romantic fiction, is also an historian, playwright, lecturer, political speaker and television personality. She has now written six hundred and eighteen books and has the distinction of holding *The Guinness Book of Records* title of the world's bestselling author, having sold over six hundred and fifty million copies of her books all over the world.

Miss Cartland is a Dame of Grace of St. John of Jerusalem; Chairman of the St. John Council in Hertfordshire; one of the first women in one thousand years ever to be admitted to the Chapter General; President of the Hertfordshire Branch of the Royal College of Midwives; President and Founder in 1964 of the National Association for Health; and invested by her Majesty the Queen as a Dame of the Order of the British Empire in 1991.

Miss Cartland lives in England at Camfield Place, Hatfield, Hertfordshire.